SARA'S FEAR

Ernie Lindsey

ISBN-13: 978-1496078148
ISBN-10: 1496078144

Sara's Fear / Ernie Lindsey. -- 1st ed.

Evil plays by its own rules.

ONE

Sara Winthrop watched as her friend and former annoying nemesis, Teddy Rutherford, picked up the fifty-pound sack of cattle feed, lifted it over the top rung of the fence, and dumped the contents into the long, blue trough.

She'd invited him and his newlywed wife out for a short visit before their real honeymoon began. Southwest Virginia was far from a month in the Caribbean, but they'd jumped at the chance to come see her new place, thousands of miles from Portland where they'd lived and worked together.

Teddy grinned and stepped away. He motioned to the cattle grazing lazily nearby. "Come on, you four-legged milk machines. Time for dinner, or supper...or whatever the hell you guys eat here in the boondocks." He glanced over at Sara. "Did I say that right? Boondocks?"

"Boonies. Sticks. Backwoods. Same thing."

"Yonder? Is that one?"

Sara chuckled. "Nice try."

He was still getting used to the southern terms, but after his second day on Sara's farm, he'd assured her

1

plenty of times that he had a handle on what it took to keep the place running. "What's that smell, Sara? Smells like…outside."

"You mean nature?"

"Yeah. That."

"It's manure and wet hay."

"You remember that guy Mark that used to work in the Testing Department?"

"Don't remind me."

"I think he wore the same thing as cologne."

"No, I sat across from Mark for three years. This is like roses compared to him."

Teddy shook his head as he stared at the cattle. They'd ambled over and buried their noses in the thick layer of feed. "Man, look at them eat. Takes a lot to keep a thousand pound hunk of beef mooing, huh?" Pointing to a large roan off to the side, he added, "Maybe when they're done, you can show me how to milk the big one over there."

Sara patted his back. "I doubt that bull would enjoy it, but you can try."

Teddy blushed and his wife, Irina, kissed him on the cheek. She said, "You stick to the business of games. Let Sara manage the cows, okay?"

Eight months earlier, Teddy's father, Jim Rutherford, had sold LightPulse Productions to a rival competitor for slightly over two billion dollars. Jim hadn't wanted to do it initially, but after the insanity with Patty Kellog, and the subsequent explosion of his home, he'd decided that maybe it was a sign that it was time for a change. He'd worked so hard to build LightPulse into an industry leader, and it had been difficult to give that up, but an extended vacation in Italy that turned into a transcontinental relocation and a swift marriage to the love of his life had softened the remorse.

Teddy had taken his share of the spoils and started his own company, called Red Mob Productions, that designed small, mindless games for mobile phones. He didn't *have* to work, would never *need* to work again, but he claimed that the desire for a challenge drove him to stay busy. Sara didn't know exactly how much he'd earned in the buyout and didn't care—it was simply good to see Teddy maturing and doing well for himself. So far, he'd turned a twenty-five million dollar investment into twenty-five million in profits. He'd done it in such a short amount of time that several gaming magazines called him the *wunderkind* of mobile development and thankfully, he hadn't allowed it go to his head.

Much.

Sara had asked him what she was supposed to do

3

with a hundred copies of *Gamemaster Magazine* that featured his smiling face on the cover, to which he'd replied, "Don't worry, I have a shipment of frames coming, too. You'll figure something out."

Sara suspected that Irina kept Teddy somewhat grounded and focused. She was good *to* him and good *for* him, and Sara told the beautiful granddaughter of a former Russian mafia general as often as she could. "You're a miracle worker," she'd said the night before, which made Irina grin and lift her wine glass, replying, "May wonders never cease."

Jim had been more than generous in divvying up the profits among his long-time managers and faithful employees. Especially with Sara, who'd earned thirty-seven million for her shares in LightPulse, in addition to the extra twenty-five million that he'd given her as part of an exit package. She'd tried to insist that it was too much, that it wasn't necessary, but the elder Rutherford would hear none of it, and threatened to give her *more* if she didn't stop with the refusal attempts.

Now, with a large portion of it donated to various charities, she had roughly forty million dollars remaining. She'd invested most of it wisely, set aside college funds for the kids, and purchased fifty acres of land adjacent to her parents' farm in southwest

Virginia. The rolling hills of the Appalachians were comforting and the kids had fit right in as soon as they set foot in the deep green grass.

Far away from the atrocities in Portland, Sara felt *new*, even though Patty Kellog was still out there somewhere. But so far, she was comfortable with their position. The farmhouse was well fortified and featured an unrivaled security system. They had acres of open land in which to see approaching visitors, both good and bad alike. Within the past week, the FBI assured her that they had a lead on Patty and it wouldn't be long.

Things had finally stabilized.

Sara's fear, lingering in the back of her mind, was that her troubles weren't really over and never would be as long as Patty and Shelley were alive, but she knew that constant worry over *possible* problems solved nothing.

Life had to move forward.

Exist, adapt, and embrace.

Embrace the day, embrace the people that matter.

Even her pesky, former arch-nemesis was welcome for a visit.

They'd been through so much together, so many unbelievable, unwanted adventures, and after years and years of hating his guts, she was proud to call him a friend. She'd saved his life. He'd saved hers. They were even.

But Teddy was still…Teddy, even under Irina's guidance. However, now Sara saw his over-confident nature more as endearing quality than an annoying nuisance.

Teddy wasn't so bad as long as you knew how to corral him.

"Looks like rain," Sara said, glancing up at the encroaching black clouds.

Teddy laughed. "You say things like that now? 'Green Acres is the place to be,' huh?"

"Goes with the territory. We should probably get back up to the house before it gets here." A gust of wind brought with it the distinct smell of rain, confirming her assessment.

"I thought you moved three thousand miles away to get away from rain."

"You know why she moved," Irina said. She patted Teddy's bottom. "To get away from *you*. Right, Sara?"

Sara winked and replied, "There's no place far enough."

"Hey, I don't *have* to be here, you know. Be nice to me. We're on our honeymoon." He tried to sound offended, but it didn't work. He shrugged and added,

"Besides, how many of these hicks keep you on your toes like I do?"

Sara turned and walked up the gravel driveway toward her home. Teddy and Irina followed. She said, "Just because they live in the middle of nowhere doesn't mean they're hicks. You'd be surprised." She pointed across the gentle, undulating hills. Spring hadn't quite sprung yet, but some of the green had returned. Off in the distance, a large log home sat nestled among a cluster of maple and oak trees. "That house belongs to a heart surgeon. The one to the right—you see it, the one with the black shingles? A former senator lives there and then behind our house, up there between those pines, that's Dr. Hayton. He's one of the top oncologists in Virginia so I think he travels more than he's home."

"What about that one? The beautiful one. It looks like a painting." Irina asked, pointing to the southwest. An old brick farmhouse with a gray roof and white-columned porch looked slightly rundown. Where Irina saw beauty, Sara saw a home that could use some work. Bricks had fallen from various spots. Vines crawled up its exterior and in the driveway, a decrepit, rusty pickup sat with its tailgate down.

"That," Sara said, "is my backup plan."

"How so?" Teddy asked.

"The guy that lives there used to be a sniper in the Marines. I haven't met him yet, but his name is Randall. If anything ever goes wrong *here*," she said, pointing at the ground beneath her feet, "I know who I'm asking for help."

Teddy stopped in the middle of the driveway. "Seriously? A sniper?"

Sara nodded. "Yeah, I guess. My folks said he had some trouble a while back. Some crazy rumors about how these hitmen were trying to kill him, but around these parts, who knows. Life moves a little slower here and people need things to talk about, so the old folks like to hang around in the local restaurants, drinking coffee and telling stories. I'm not sure which they do more of, to be honest."

Teddy grinned. "People were trying to kill him?"

Irina added, "If that's true, isn't it dangerous to be so close?"

"Everything's seemed fine over there. Quiet. And like I said, it's probably just old folks gossiping. I've met his wife and little boy before. She's a bit rough around the edges but their son is an absolute sweetheart. Her sister, Mary, is a private investigator and former officer, too. I'm surrounded by good company."

"Sounds like it," Teddy said. "Do you think we

could go talk to him later?"

A fat drop of rain smacked Sara on the forehead.

"Maybe. Why?" She resumed her hike back up the short hill. Looking to the southwest, she could see the black clouds creeping in, blocking out the blue sky.

Teddy and Irina stayed close behind. He said, "We're doing a new first-person shooter called *Sniper One* and it's already getting major buzz. We're not even halfway through development yet and some reporters are calling it the next big thing. I mean, you should see the graphics, Sara. They're totally unreal for a smartphone."

"And what does this have to do with Randall?"

"I don't know. Research. It might be fun to sit down and talk to him, maybe pour him a beer and ask a few questions. We've hired some consultants—these former enlisted guys—so we could be solid on our accuracy, right? But all those dudes want to talk about is physics and trajectories and shit I don't understand in the slightest. What I'm looking for is the *story* behind it all. I couldn't care less if a bullet follows a certain flight path in windy conditions over a half mile on a random Tuesday in rural freakin' Afghanistan. What I want to know is…what's the story behind the target? How'd the sniper get there? Why does the dude he's shooting at…why does he have to die? Narratives. Not math and science. Remember how we used to argue over that stuff?"

Irina squeezed his hand. "Somebody dared to argue with you? I don't believe it."

"Yeah. Sara and I used to have some epic battles back in the day."

"And I always won," Sara informed Irina. "Didn't I, Little One?"

Teddy threw his head back and cackled. "Jesus, I haven't heard that in ages."

They laughed harder at Irina's confused look and explained the insulting term of endearment. "I can't say I miss those days, Teddy, but seriously, it's good to see you doing so well. And thanks for coming to visit." She put her arm around his shoulder. The gesture didn't feel quite so foreign anymore. "Being here, with my parents right over the hill…it's nice to have family so close and some peace, but we miss our friends, though, and the kids ask about you and your dad quite a bit."

"They do?"

"Once they found out you were coming, that's all they talked about." Sara climbed up the front porch steps. Teddy came next, then Irina.

Sara peeked through the living room window. Inside, Miss Willow sat reading a book. When Sara had decided to move, there was no question that the soft-spoken, flower-child babysitter was coming with them. She didn't need to ask, and neither did Miss Willow.

Sara gently rapped on the window.

Miss Willow looked up, waved, and then turned a page.

Teddy flopped down into a rocking chair. Irina took the one next to him, Sara settled into the third. She zipped her windbreaker higher as the chilly gust of wind pushed through.

Teddy said, "That's awesome to hear, Sara. Thanks for that."

"You're welcome. It's the truth. They ask about Barker, too, but I haven't talked to him in about two weeks. There for a while, right after we left, he called every other day to make sure we were fine."

Teddy planted both feet to stop the rocking chair. "Wait…you haven't heard?"

"Heard what?"

He glanced sideways at Irina, who put a hand over her mouth.

"Heard what, Teddy?"

"I thought for sure you knew and I wondered why you hadn't brought it up. Barker got shot a couple of weeks ago and he's been in the hospital since then. He'll be fine but it was kinda iffy there for a while."

Sara leaned up, hands on her knees. "Oh my God, what happened?"

"Normal follow-up on this case he was working. I can't remember what it was, but he went through a door and bam-bam, one in his side," Teddy said, pointing down near his waist, "and then another one went in right under his ribcage. Well, actually, it clipped the bone and ricocheted off. They think that's what saved his life."

"And he's going to make it?"

"Yeah, but I doubt he's going back to work. He'll live, but the bullet did quite a bit of damage when it plowed through there."

"That's *insane*. I mean, holy crap, I wondered why he hadn't called. Did you go see him in the hospital? Did they catch who did it?"

Teddy said to Irina, "Hon, see if you can find that article online. The one with the two pics, remember?"

"Which one?"

"The one with him in a uniform beside the one where he's in his hospital bed."

"Right, okay."

While Irina scanned through news articles on her phone, Teddy explained what he knew as dollops of rain began to pepper the porch roof.

Irina gasped and tapped Teddy on the shoulder.

She handed her phone to him. "Look," she said.

"Did you find it?"

"No, read this."

Teddy scanned the screen, reading to himself. Sara watched his lips move. The expression on Irina's face worried her, too.

"What is it?" Sara said.

"Unbelievable."

"What? Tell me."

"They had a riot at Coffee Creek this morning."

Coffee Creek Correctional Facility was the place that Shelley Sergeant had called home for the past two years. "Let me see that." Sara reached over and snatched the phone from Teddy's hand, then read the article out loud. "Inmates escape after early morning riot. Local officials are still trying to figure out exactly what incited the riot at Coffee Creek Correctional Facility at four o'clock this morning...blah blah...unsubstantiated rumors report that witnesses heard a small explosion before the riot began... No comment... The only thing that Warden Bill Keller would confirm is that there are at least two dead and four missing who are presumed to have escaped. Authorities are advising residents not to open their doors for strangers... Identities and pictures of the escaped will be released as soon as they're confirmed… More details to follow."

Teddy said, "Sara, you don't think…"

Her hands were numb. She shook her head. "If she escaped, three thousand miles is a long way…right?"

TWO

3:59AM
Wilsonville, Oregon
Coffee Creek Correctional Facility

Patty Kellog, also known as Boudica and former leader of the now defunct terrorist group called The Clan, stood to the west of the small prison. She was dressed in black, head to toe, providing perfect cover in the darkness. The three men behind her wore identical outfits matching hers. Each carried an Uzi and a shoulder strap flush with grenades. They were practically invisible under the thin tree line.

She listened to the far off rumble of an approaching train. It would give them good noise cover and a good distraction upon their approach. She shifted her balance from one foot to the next and waited for the train to come closer.

Months ago, when Patty had visited Shelley Sergeant for the first time, with her deceased bomb technician known as Quirk, she'd promised the young, sadistic talent that she would have her freedom in two years.

Plans, and motivations, changed.

There was a sense of urgency brought about by frustration and impatience, then delayed by the need to find decent men willing to work with her. It seemed as if Vadim Bariskov, the Spirit, had more pull in the international community than she realized. Although they had escaped from Jim Rutherford's home together, through the secret tunnel and seconds before the bomb detonated, she realized too late that it had been a mistake to let him live.

If she had known how quickly his loose tongue could spread misinformation, she would've slit his throat and watched his body float away through Portland's drainage system. Instead, they'd parted ways with the assurance that it was easier to escape as individuals rather than as a team.

She hadn't seen him since. The Spirit had vanished, as he was known to do. Then, when she began the laborious process of recruiting a new squad, words like "careless" and "inept" were suggested, along with phrases such as, "loose cannon" and "unpredictable, impulsive neophyte," which hindered her recruitment tactics over and over again. For months, she had traveled the world, enduring cockroach-infested motels in Thailand, sleazy bestiality bars in South America, and a moose-themed restaurant in Canada, looking, asking, and hunting for anyone willing to work with her soiled reputation. It took some work and more promises than she could keep, but she'd finally settled on the D-list assassins with her now.

Patty glanced at the three men standing nearby. They weren't the best, but they were affordable, and that would have to do. She shook her head. If she ever came across the Spirit again, retribution wouldn't be an option—it would be a guarantee.

The rumbling of the freight train grew louder. Patty held up a hand. "Hold," she said. "Just a little more." At three hundred yards, they had plenty of time.

The man closest to her, Jensen, fidgeted and moved a step nearer to the tracks. He'd expressed his concerns about her plan, chief among them the need to dart in front of a moving behemoth weighing millions of pounds.

Patty clenched her teeth. "I said *hold*."

Jensen flashed a look over his left shoulder and said, "I'm not waiting." He readjusted his grip on the Uzi and broke into a run, ducking low and beneath the single headlight.

Patty didn't vacillate. She dropped Jensen with an accurate shot to the calf. He yelped, fell, and rolled to the side, clutching his leg. He barely had a chance to get his arms up before she was on top of him. A muffled *chuff* escaped the silencer of her compact 9mm, leaving a single hole in the center of his forehead.

What a waste. He had potential, but she couldn't risk him accidentally sabotaging the mission any further. At least she hadn't paid him yet. Silver linings, they say.

She quickly tried to gauge the train's distance. Two hundred yards, easy. More than likely, the engineers hadn't seen anything from that far away. Jensen's body alongside the tracks would be nothing but a black lump and it was doubtful they'd even notice.

Crenley and Tanner crouched behind her, breathing quietly, waiting patiently.

"Orders, ma'am?" Tanner asked, with no regard to his fallen associate.

Patty looked at the rugged face covered in camo paint, studying the emotionless eyes. She thought she could grow to like this one. He had the right attitude. Beside him, Crenley spat a mouthful of tobacco juice onto Jensen's leg.

Crenley said, "He was weak," and then looked at the approaching train. "What now?"

Patty smiled. She'd made the right choice with these two. She signaled for them to follow her as they sprinted through the underbrush, hopping stray limbs and shallow crevices. She nearly rolled an ankle on a small rock but recovered well and kept moving. Patty stopped at the tracks and held up a hand. She checked her watch. "Train's early, but we need to move. You ready?"

Both nodded.

"Then keep your head down. This should be easy."

***

That was an hour ago.

Should.

Should've been easy.

She should've known.

Tanner screamed in the backseat, the bullet wound in his stomach bleeding slowly but sure to kill him if they didn't get help soon. Crenley swiped at the sweat on his forehead and resumed the pressure on Tanner's leaking gut.

Crenley said, "We gotta get him some help."

Patty checked the rearview mirror. "Where? Huh? Where?"

SARA'S FEAR

Shelley Sergeant sat in the passenger's seat, grinning, and occasionally looking out the windows. "I don't see anybody coming."

Crenley said to Patty, "He'll die if we don't."

"What the hell do you expect me to do? Maybe I should stop at 7-11 and get him a couple of cotton swabs. Would that work?"

"Kill him," Shelley suggested.

"No, don't."

Patty shook her head. "We need him. He's good."

"He'll slow us down."

Patty checked the side mirrors again. She leaned over and scanned the sky above, expecting to see a hovering helicopter with a searchlight. Nothing. Why weren't they chasing after them? Was it manpower issues? Did they alert the local police? The FBI? Coffee Creek was comprised of both minimum and medium-security populations, but it still didn't mean that they would've ignored a full-fledged escape. Especially not after Tanner tossed a grenade at a wall as a last resort.

Things had gone wrong from the start. The first guard she'd bribed appeared at the southwest corner without Shelley, insisting that it had been impossible to get her out. He got two bullets in the chest; one for his cowardice and one for his inability to perform. Their backup plan didn't work as well as expected either.

Inside the prison walls, the second bribed guard was supposed to create a distraction—a difficult task at four o'clock in the morning.

His "distraction" had turned into a riot. He'd managed to call Patty and give brief details before she heard a loud *thunk*, followed by the sound of a phone skittering across the floor.

Next came Tanner's grenade opening a hole in the wall. Smoke. Fires. Burning mattresses. Screaming women fighting, pulling hair, beating disoriented guards with batons and table legs. Blood and gunfire. Tanner screaming. Crenley returning sporadic, peppered shots.

Somehow, throughout the raging chaos of flashing red lights and drifting banks of gray smoke, Patty found Shelley Sergeant in the middle of a hallway. She stood with her arms crossed, watching the carnage and smiling like a kid at Disney World.

Patty had grabbed her, offered a simple "Remember me?" and then they'd all retreated with Shelley in tow. Maybe amongst the insanity, the guards were disoriented and trying to regain control. Maybe they hadn't yet realized that one of their inmates was missing. She tried to recall if any of the night guards— the ones that had lived—had seen them escaping through the crumbling gash in the wall.

Was it possible they hadn't been spotted? Perhaps. Perhaps not.

If the gods were on her side, and they usually were, they'd made it out cleanly and the search for the missing inmate wouldn't commence until the authorities performed a headcount.

How long did they have? A couple of hours at the most? The interior of the prison was in complete disarray, total madness, and she couldn't imagine that the prison officials would get things under control quickly enough to do a live pursuit.

At best, reports would emerge regarding a shadowy commando team, followed by Shelley's face on every news channel. There would be reporters and press conferences. Officials imploring residents to be on the lookout for a one-eyed blonde escapee. Hotlines would receive hundreds of calls.

It would happen, but not for a while.

They'd gotten lucky. They were away, clean, for the time being.

Now, hurtling along the interstate, Patty looked over at the excited blonde wearing the prison *chic* orange jumpsuit. The young woman would need to lose the eye patch, definitely. It was too identifying, too conspicuous. She might as well have had a tattoo on her face like Mike Tyson.

Crenley said, "We're losing him. Come on, do something."

Lights from an oncoming rig swept across his face in the back seat. Patty could see the anger and desperation in his bulging eyes and pursed lips. Tanner and Crenley had come as a package deal—longtime partners who'd worked hundreds of off-the-record missions together for the CIA. Black ops assignments in South America, Sudan, and North Korea, plus many more than they'd cared to mention. When Uncle Sam had sent them on their way, without pensions or acknowledgment, it had left a bitter taste. For the past five years, they'd happily worked for anyone who considered themselves an enemy of any state. Freedom fighters, guerrilla warlords, it didn't matter as long as the paycheck had enough zeroes behind it.

"Fine," Patty said, whipping the battered Ford Explorer to the right and down an exit ramp where she plowed over the stop sign and took a hard right turn. She wrenched the steering wheel to the left and dropped the SUV back onto all four tires. Up ahead, the searing lights of a McDonald's parking lot brightened everything within reach.

She careened into the lot and sped around to the back of the restaurant.

"What're you doing?" Crenley asked. "I said we

need *help*, you dumb shit."

Tires squealed as she slammed on the brakes and pitched everyone forward.

Patty felt the gun barrel behind her right ear before she could shift the car into park.

Crenley growled. "Hospital. Now."

"This is so much fun." Shelley giggled and clapped.

Patty slammed the gearshift up and took her foot off the brakes. "We *do not* have time for this bullshit, Crenley. I'll make you a deal," Patty said. "Take your partner and throw him in that dumpster. Get rid of him and I'll pay you double."

"No."

"Triple and you stay on with me. I have more work coming."

Silence from the back seat. Patty could sense his indecision. Was he thinking it over? Was he weighing the possible scenarios? Bullet in her head, then one in Shelley? Then what?

She eased her 9mm across the bench-style front seat as deftly as possible until it was within Shelley's reach, calmly waving a hand back and forth to get her attention. As soon as Shelley glanced down, Patty said, "Crenley? Look at me, okay? Look. What did we agree on, huh? Fifty thousand for tonight and an escort to

Virginia? I'll tell you what—make it five hundred if you stay with me through the end of this job. You might have fun with it anyway."

"Five hundred thousand? You're serious?"

"Tanner goes in the dumpster with an extra bullet, you come with us to see the rest of our mission through, and you're half a mil richer. Sound good?"

She watched his eyes darting back and forth. Crenley lowered the gun from her ear. The spot where the barrel had been on her skin stayed cool. When he looked away once more, she risked a peek and saw that Shelley was prepared.

"What do you say, Crenley? We could use your help."

Tanner moaned and mumbled something that sounded like, "Cold."

She watched in the rearview mirror as Crenley breathed deeply, huffed, and then shook his head. "I don't think I can do—"

Beside her: *chuff-chuff.*

Shelley giggled as Crenley slumped over. She leaned across the front seat and put a finishing touch on Tanner. *Chuff.* One in the forehead.

Patty liked this girl, for damn sure, more than she liked the two mediocre assassins in the back leaking blood that they'd have to clean up later.

Shelley said, "God, that felt good. It's been too long."

THREE

Sara stood in the living room of her farmhouse, watching the headline ticker run along the bottom of the CNN broadcast. "Nothing new," she said, chewing on a fingernail. "Give me something." Three hours had passed and they continued to offer the same information. There was a prison riot in Oregon, two guards were dead, and four inmates were presumed missing. The last she'd heard, the local authorities were finalizing the headcount just to be sure.

All fires were out in the prison and several of the inmates had been escorted to the infirmary for injuries and the effects of smoke inhalation. Additional doctors were on site to conduct medical examinations and treatment. Any further information was pending the press conference at five o'clock eastern time.

Sara wasn't sure she could wait two more hours. The tips of her fingers would be bloody nubs by that time. Thankfully, the kids were home from their mid-week early release day, and they sat in the entertainment room with Teddy and Irina, watching something on the Disney Channel.

Miss Willow brought Sara a mug of chamomile

tea. "Something to soothe your nerves, dear."

"Thanks." Sara blew into the mug and took a sip. A touch of cream, just the way she liked it. Over the past couple of years, Miss Willow had nearly become as much of a sitter to Sara as she was the children.

"Anything?"

"Not a word," Sara said. "There's a press conference at five. Hopefully by then they'll have the headcount finished and we can see who escaped."

"Supposedly," Miss Willow reminded her. "*Unaccounted for* doesn't mean that the Sergeant girl is in an airplane and on her way here."

"Or, that's exactly what it means."

Miss Willow put her arm around Sara's waist and pulled her close. Sara rested her head against the taller woman's shoulder. It was comforting in the absence of her mother and father, who'd taken their annual Carnival cruise to the Bahamas at the perfectly wrong time. Miss Willow was an excellent security blanket and deserved every bit of credit for keeping Sara sane for the past twenty-four months, but nothing could replace the warm embrace of a concerned, caring parent.

Sara thought about how ridiculous it was to revert to some childish sense of dependency. She was in her mid-thirties, for God's sake, Mommy and Daddy wouldn't be around to protect her forever. In spite of this, it didn't change the fact that being comforted by a parent that loved you remained a good emotional stabilizer.

"Now, now," Miss Willow said. "I'm going to steal one of Barker's expressions for a second. What's the one? He says, 'Don't borrow trouble because the interest is too high.' Okay?"

Sara pulled free of the embrace and walked over to the couch. She sat, took a sip of her tea, then covered her eyes. "I know... This is so ridiculous. Why am I worrying about it?" She grunted, then answered her own question. "I'll tell you why, because she's insane enough to try something like this. I mean, Jesus, the FBI said they had a possible lead on Patty Kellog, but she's out there somewhere because they never found her body. What if the both of them are teaming up to hunt me down?"

Miss Willow rolled her eyes.

Sara chuckled. "Think about it, Willow. Huh? Am I crazy? Crap like that runs through my head in the middle of the night."

Miss Willow switched off the television, then shut the front door and locked it. Using the keypad near the door, she armed the multiple security systems; alarms beeped, LED displays flashed, and colors went from red to green. "There. Happy now?"

"It helps."

Miss Willow pointed a scolding finger at her and said, "And when are you going to change that pass code, huh? I've been telling you for months now that you can't use the same one for everything, especially one that you've been using for years. It's too dangerous."

"I know, I know. An ounce of prevention. I'll get to it." Sara sighed and nudged up to the edge of the couch. "Honestly, are we safe here?" She lowered her voice, flicking her chin toward the entertainment room. "Are the *kids* safe here?"

Teddy entered the room from the opposite direction, spooking Sara. Evidently he'd gone through the entertainment room, into the kitchen, and then popped in via the other side. She jumped. He apologized, then said, "Miss Willow's right, you know. Don't borrow trouble."

"Were you listening the whole time?"

He nodded. "Sorry. Jacob wanted a snack. Couldn't help but overhear because I spent so much damn time trying to find the candy he was asking for. What're you feeding those guys, huh? *Kale chips*? Really?"

"Mind your own," Sara said, feeling the gentle

roots of a smile growing. "It has to be stuff like kale chips or Jacob will eat every sweet thing in the house."

"Right. Anyway." Teddy squeezed Sara's shoulder. "You okay?"

"I'm…no, I'm not. Not until I hear that Shelley's part of the headcount."

"You gotta trust the system, Sara. You're in Virginia for Christ's sake. Even if she did manage to get out and get away, they'll find her. She'll turn up in some roadside motel in who-knows-where Arizona. You see it on the news all the time, right? They usually find these people a few miles down the road because they were dumb enough to head back to their ex-girlfriend's house instead of making a smart decision for the first time in their lives. And keep in mind, the lack of smart decisions are what got them there in the first place."

"True, but you're forgetting one thing."

"What's that?"

"Shelley was a genius."

"And you beat her, and she's in prison. What does that tell you?"

Sara wasn't sure it told her that much. She'd been smart enough to get through the levels of Shelley's game, smart enough to figure out that insane puzzle with only a couple of seconds remaining, and smart enough to best Shelley overall, but was it a fluke? Anybody with enough deductive reasoning could've figured that out, couldn't they? Was she really smarter, and better, than Shelley? Not necessarily. "It tells me," she said, "that I got lucky. One good guess doesn't mean I'm the superhero to her supervillain."

"Come here," Teddy said, playing rough, pulling her up from the couch and hugging her. He used his knuckles to scrub her head like an annoying little brother. She laughed, twisted his nipple, and pulled away.

"You're ridiculous. Don't make me laugh, Teddy. I'm scared, I want to be pissed off."

"Sara, dude, take a deep breath. Miss Willow, will you tell her to relax? What did you tell me earlier, huh? You've got a *three hundred thousand* dollar security system on this house. Bulletproof glass. A panic room down in the basement that you modeled after Dad's, and enough cameras posted around the property to film a squirrel taking a dump. I'm sure the guy monitoring all the feeds out of here is gonna love that, by the way."

Despite her concern and her need to obsess, Sara had to admit that Teddy was right and being rational. Somewhat. She'd never tell him to his face, obviously—can't give the little bastard too much room for his head to grow—but it was nice to have him around to provide some validity to the obvious. *Rational* and *Teddy* in the same breath. The world had surely turned upside down.

"Let's go have some fun," he said. "We'll relax a little bit, then come back and watch the press conference in a couple of hours, and everything will be fine, okay? Now, it sounds like the kids are done with their movie and I need to get Irina out of there before she decides she wants some of those little buggers running around the house."

Miss Willow said, "I'll go get a snack for them."

"I ate all the kale chips," Teddy said. "Not really. They went down the garbage disposal."

Sara stood and flicked his earlobe. "Jerk. Do you know how much those things actually cost when you can find them here in the country?"

"Whatever it is, I'm sure they're not worth it."

***

Irina had decided to stay behind and play with the children, which had given Teddy plenty of reason to complain on the way down to the neighbor's house. However, there was a hint of acquiescence in his voice. He said, "I don't know what's gotten into her lately, but that's all she talks about, Sara. Kids, babies. The other day I caught her online researching college savings funds. I'm telling you, put a thermometer in that woman's mouth and her baby fever would be up near one-oh-five."

"When did that start?"

"After her birthday two weeks ago."

"Ah." Sara nodded, knowingly. "How old? She's thirty, right? Couple of years younger than you?"

"Yeah."

"I know it's such a ridiculous cliché, but the biological clock ticks louder around that age. She's ready."

"*I'm* not."

"You sure?"

Teddy looked away to hide his grin. The rain had dissipated to a light misty drizzle. The smell of wet earth wafted up and off in the distance, just above the row of pine trees on top of Greenwood Hill, a speckle of blue sky poked through the clouds. He said, "I put on a good show, but…yeah. Maybe." He latched onto Sara's arm and squeezed softly. "Don't you dare tell her that, okay? Not yet. I'm getting there, but I don't want to start tomorrow. We've got the release of *Sniper One* coming up, I'm on the road all the time…it's a lot to handle."

"I don't know if there's every a right time, Teddy.

People plan for children, I guess, but you never really know how much your world is going to turn upside down until you're right in the thick of it. Read all the books you want—get prepared, buy things that you'll never use like cute, pinkish changing table straps that hold the changing pad where it's supposed to go, but you never know until you're right there, holding that screaming baby with breast milk on your shirt and poop in your hair that you've made the right choice."

"So, you're actually trying to *encourage* me with the idea of poop in my hair?"

Sara laughed and entered the security code to open the gate at the end of her driveway. When it swung closed, she again tapped the numbers on the access panel and listened to the latches slide into place, along with the heavy metal bars that secured it to the driveway underneath it. Nothing was getting through there short of a tank. The perimeter fence could use some reinforcement, she knew, but those alterations weren't set to be made until the following month. She'd debated it for days, not wanting to ruin the aesthetics of the countryside, but, if she and the kids weren't alive to enjoy them, the eyesore wouldn't matter anyway.

Maybe. She was still…on the fence, so to speak.

Sara continued, "Brian and I weren't sure we

wanted kids. Not at first. Realists like me, or you for that matter, we get so caught up in the way the world is that it's hard to imagine subjecting a child to all this crap that's on the news everyday. Brian and I were sure we'd rather keep a child safe from that by *not* having one than by having one and trying to protect it."

"So why did you?"

Sara shrugged. "Oops." She checked the winding country road for traffic and stepped across to the other side. Gravel had washed down from the Halloran's driveway up the hill, leaving a layer of loose gravel across the hardtop. In the field to their left, a collection of rocks and pebbles had gathered like a small creek bed.

"*Oops?* Lacey and Callie were…what's the plural of *oops?* Oopses? Oopsi?"

"I don't know if it matters anymore—whoa, don't step in that."

Teddy narrowly avoided a cow patty in the middle of the road, nimbly sidestepping in mid-stride.

Sara continued, "You know, it doesn't matter, to be honest. Oops or no oops, your world changes, and you go from panic so strong that you've got pee running down your leg to be the happiest you've ever been, with someone else's pee running down your leg. When it's one of those days where you've got breast milk on the ceiling and you haven't slept in twenty-four hours, you survive with a smile. It's an amazing thing, Teddy. It really is."

"Sara, come on. You know how I am."

"You've changed."

"I have?"

"Irina's changed you. You've changed yourself. And God, I'm sure that was like turning a battleship around—"

"Hey!"

"Even like, two years ago, Teddy, you know? Before that crazy stuff with Shelley, I wouldn't have trusted you to babysit a fish tank for the weekend, but now, you've made it, my boy. Welcome to adulthood."

"Against my better judgment, I'll take that as a compliment. Still doesn't mean that I'm ready for a baby even though I get to sit at the adult table."

"It'll happen when it happens. And, it'll probably make Irina feel better if you tell her that you're ready…you're just not *tomorrow* ready."

"You sure?"

"Communication, bud. That's the best path to take."

"Right." They stopped by the silver mailbox with black, stenciled lettering that read, "Blevins, Route 2 Box 742," though the "E" was missing in "Route."

Teddy asked, "Did you let this guy know we were coming?"

"No. Around here, people show up on your front porch, whether you asked them to or not. My parents say it's a southern thing. It took some getting used to, but it helps when you have a surveillance system, too."

"You said this dude was an ex-sniper, though. He's not going to shoot us walking up to his house, is he?"

Sara marched up the long, winding gravel driveway. She looked over her shoulder and motioned for Teddy to follow. "*You* maybe, but I'm hoping he'll recognize me."

"And that's supposed to be comforting?"

"Yes."

Reluctantly, Teddy followed.

FOUR

Patty drove along the narrow, snow-covered road, creeping through the campground, searching for any brave souls willing to test their mettle against the cold, dreary Oregon winters. High in the Cascades, the white blanket was thick and wet.

Surely, some bearded hippie with his crunchy wife would be tucked back in a secluded corner. She and Shelley hadn't driven too far out, away from the McDonald's, before finding a campground sign. Although it read, "Closed for the Season," she knew that it was merely a marker, signifying that the state wouldn't maintain upkeep until the spring. It didn't prevent the diehard nature lovers from staying a few miserable nights.

Shelley rolled down her window and stuck her head out. She inhaled deeply.

"What're you doing?" Patty asked.

"That's what freedom smells like." Shelley leaned back inside the SUV and began rolling the window up. Pausing halfway, she whispered, "Stop. Stop! Over there. Look."

A green tent, small and triangular, big enough for

one or two people only, sat nestled in between a heavy cluster of pine saplings that provided good cover against the wind. Natural and unnatural shelter coexisting. The tent looked old, worn down, and for a moment, Patty thought it might've been abandoned until she noticed the thin sliver of smoke drifting up from the remnants of a campfire.

Above it and hanging from a limb was an orange backpack, what looked to be a bag of food, and then another backpack next to it. Patty was hoping for a female hiker or camper, someone about Shelley's size so they could get her out of the screamingly obvious prison jumpsuit. She hoped she'd found what they were looking for because the second backpack was fluorescent pink.

The sun was up and Patty wondered how long it would be before the campers were as well. How should they play the situation? Approach while the couple slept and catch them off guard? That was the wisest choice. They were miles from civilization. Out here, there would be no one to hear them scream except the animals.

Or…should they snatch the campers, then tie them up in the back of the Explorer? Would hostages be good bargaining power or a burden and complete distraction? One never knew when she would need a human shield.

No, it wasn't worth the trouble. Hostages meant visibility. Hostages, if you didn't plan to kill them, had memories and voices. The private flight she'd booked out of the city of Bend was scheduled for nine o'clock. In three hours, she and Shelley would be on their way across the U.S. to an Appalachian mountain town called Marion, Virginia. That was the thing about private flights: unregulated and unburdened by NTSB rules, you could have a suitcase nuke in your luggage and travel from one spot to the next with less scrutiny than the guy in security busting your chops over a shaving cream can that was larger than three ounces.

From Bend, they would make one quick stop in Minnesota to refuel and then land in a regional airport close to Bristol, Tennessee. Patty had grown up in northern Virginia and had spent the early part of her life there before she had left for the home-away-from-home mental hospital, so she was familiar with Bristol. That's where her uncle Marty used to travel to watch NASCAR races. Marion, on the other hand, she remembered as being a blip on the map while they hurtled past on I-81. However, there were water towers alongside the interstate with gigantic words painted on the side that read "HOT" and "COLD" which her father thought was the funniest thing he'd ever seen.

There were times, like when she was slitting the throat of the man she loved in Prague, that she missed the life she'd once had. Vacations with her parents in Gatlinburg, Tennessee and Kitty Hawk, North Carolina, visiting with relatives in Nashville and Atlanta. Those were simpler days. She'd miss them long enough to recall slipping poison into her parents' coffee—retribution for sending her away—before she'd shake her head free of the nostalgia.

Sentimental reminiscing weakened resolve.

Close the box. Lock it. Throw it into the sun.

Watch it burn.

"I see movement," Shelley said.

Patty blinked and refocused. Drifting off like that was dangerous. She'd have to be more careful now that she had the burgeoning talent of Shelley Sergeant riding shotgun. She liked what she'd seen so far, but the young woman was unpredictable. Space out like that again and she might find that Shelley had a knife at her throat.

The zipper on the tent slowly rose up and out poked the head of a sleepy-eyed camper.

Patty said, "You got a t-shirt on under there?"

"Yeah."

"Get rid of the orange. Pull it down to your waist."

"Why? Aren't we going to kill whoever it is anyway?"

"We don't want to spook them. Spooked people run, and I'm too tired to chase somebody through the snow out here."

"Whatever." Shelley wriggled out of the top half of her prison attire and tied the sleeves around her waist.

When the man emerged from the tent, Patty saw that his bushy beard hung a foot down from his cheeks and chin. The red, knitted skullcap sat at an awkward angle. He squinted against the morning sun and waved before climbing out.

Patty shut off the engine. They must've been an odd sight, sitting there in an idling vehicle and staring, miles from anywhere. "Roll your window down all the way. Be friendly," she said to Shelley. Then, as the man approached, she said, "Morning."

"How's it going?" His voice was cheerful with a younger pitch than what his beard suggested. The skin around his eyes was taut without a hint of crow's feet. When he was back at the tent, Patty would've guessed early forties, but up close, he was maybe twenty-one. "Can I help you guys?"

Before Patty could offer a sociable response,

Shelley bluntly asked, "What's with your packs in the trees?"

Patty rolled her eyes. Shelley was too impetuous. There would have to be a discussion about that.

"Um...for the animals. You know, to keep them from trying to raid the tent. Bears mostly." He blew on his hands and rubbed them together.

"Oh. Makes sense."

"You guys looking for a place to post up?"

"Maybe," Patty said. "Is this a good area?"

The young man shoved his hands in his front pockets and shrugged. "Depends on what you're looking for, I guess. Peace and quiet? Yeah, it's awesome."

Patty smiled. "Is that what you're doing? Getting away from it all?"

He lowered his eyes to the ground. A little red crept into his cheeks as he looked back over his shoulder, toward the tent. "Not really."

"No?"

"We're...we're field researchers. Biologists, actually, looking for signs of...um... signs of Sasquatch, honestly."

Shelley laughed. "No shit? Have you found anything?"

"Maybe." The guy grinned and winked.

Behind him, Patty saw a blonde head poke out between the tent flaps. A young woman, around the same age as their new friend, looked over and then crawled out. She wore a puffy red jacket, a headband covering her ears, and what looked to be skintight ski pants. Her feet were tucked into those ugly brown boots that all the girls her age wore. Despite her choice of footwear, she was cute.

"Hi," she called over. "I'm Chrissy." She trudged through the snow and approached the Explorer.

"Right, and I'm Denny," the guy said, sticking his hand into the open window. Shelley shook it, and so did Patty.

"How long have you guys been out here?"

"Just for the night so far. We scheduled a three-day stay, but we expected more of the snow to be gone."

Chrissy kissed his cheek. "*He* did. I knew better."

"But," Denny said, glancing around at the ground, "it'll be easer to find tracks and trails in the snow. If we can handle the cold, we'll probably stay the whole time."

Patty thought about how perfect the opportunity could've been. Chrissy was roughly the size of Shelley, so there'd be clothes to change into. These two were here in the middle of nowhere, scheduled to be out long enough so that no one would come looking for them until it was too late.

But Denny had made an excellent point. Tracks would be easy to follow. They couldn't necessarily shoot them and then hide the bodies somewhere in the woods. Four sets of prints. Blood in the snow. Tire tracks that could be loosely matched to the make and model of their SUV.

Then, Chrissy said something that sealed their fates.

"The weather report said they're expecting another eight to twelve inches tonight or tomorrow, so we're thinking we might pack up and try again later in the spring. If you guys were looking to stay around here, it might be a better idea to go back down to a lower elevation where it's not so—"

Chuff. Chuff.

Two shots. Denny and Chrissy slumped and dropped to the ground.

Shelley smiled at Patty and blew across the top of the silencer like an Old West gunslinger.

Patty grabbed her arm and yanked. "Are you kidding me?"

"What? That's what you wanted, right?"

"Yes, but you *have* to start showing some control, okay? This isn't some game where you can just run around popping people and not expect there to be any consequences. I don't care how careless you are with *your* life, but if you're going to work *with* me and *for* me, we need some boundaries. Some rules. I'm not going to prison because you feel like you're free to do whatever the hell you want. Do you understand?"

Shelley scoffed and pulled her arm free. "Yes, *Mom*. And who says I'm working *for* you?"

Patty grabbed a handful of Shelley's hair and jerked her across the cab. Face to face, nearly nose touching nose, she said, "Let me be perfectly clear. I got you out of prison. I risked my ass to save yours. If it weren't for me, you'd be in there rotting with the rest of the pond scum."

"You're hurting—"

"Shut up." Patty shook her. "You are *mine*. There are no other options. You're mine, you work for me, or you're dead. Got it?"

"I guess…"

"There's no guessing. I own you. You work for me now. We're professionals, damn it, and you're going to start acting like it." Patty shoved her away.

Shelley curled up a lip and rubbed the side of her head.

"Now get your ass out here and help me clean up your stupid mess. Get that pink bag down and find some clothes. Bodies go in the tent, and then we'll see if there's anything to eat. Easy enough?"

"Yes."

"Good. Try not to shoot anything else." Patty slung open the door and stepped out into the cold. The two biologists had either been brave or stupid to tackle their project at this elevation and in this temperature; whichever one it was, they were also unlucky to have been in the wrong place at the wrong time. So it goes.

The meek shall inherit the earth?

Not when the predators have better weapons.

Patty stomped around to the right side of the Explorer while Shelley got out, stepped over the bodies, and then marched through the snow. Patty kneeled down and tried to survey the damage. She lifted the female's head, then the male's. The bullets had gone through on both. Patty wondered if there would be metal fragments and if it would be worth doing a quick scan of the snow. The answers were possibly, and probably not. By noon, they'd be so far away that it wouldn't matter.

Shelley, having retrieved the pink backpack, slinked toward the tent.

"No, hey," Patty said to her. "Bodies first. Don't get blood on whatever you're going to change into."

"I know that." Shelley slung the backpack to the tent's side, and kicked her way through the snow. "Aren't you going to help me?"

Patty considered telling her to do it her damn self, just to teach her a lesson, but their schedule did have some limitations. "You get under the arms, I'll get the legs."

Two minutes later, they'd dragged the bodies inside the tent and zipped it closed. With any luck, the two of them wouldn't be found for days.

Shelley stripped in the frigid, open air as Patty worked on burying the blood with snow, twigs, and dirt. She looked back and watched as Shelley stood silently, nude, arms extended to the side, with her head turned up to the sun. She was smiling, breathing deeply.

Strange girl, Patty thought.

She hoped she hadn't made a mistake.

FIVE

Sara sipped at her coffee and leaned back against the kitchen counter. She watched the interaction between the miniscule Teddy Rutherford and the massive Randall Blevins. It reminded her of that old Looney Tunes cartoon with that tiny dog, Chester, yapping in the face of the gruff bulldog, Spike.

However, Randall seemed friendlier than Spike, and happily answered Teddy's questions. Well, *happily* might've been a bit of a stretch. Randall, amused, endured her former coworker's never-ending stream of inquiries about life as a sniper and what it took to spend days out in the bush, waiting and lying immobile with such patience that a snake could crawl across his neck.

"You really did that?" Teddy asked.

Randall gave a short, humble nod. "Yup. It's a story for another day, but my spotter didn't fare so well when it happened to him."

"Man, we've gotta work that into the plotline somehow."

Sara set her mug down on the counter and checked her watch. They'd been there for thirty minutes already, and she was anxious to get back and watch the news even though the press conference wouldn't start for another hour. As the two men talked, she listened to their chatter and surveyed Randall's kitchen. The Blevins abode could certainly use some updating. The linoleum was worn and discolored in spots. The flooring sagged slightly in the middle, and some of the cabinetry seemed to be out of flush. One cabinet door looked newer than the rest.

Across the counter and into the open area of the dining room, the paneling had a faded rectangle where a picture had once hung, larger than the one of Randall's family that hung there now. Like she'd mentioned to Teddy, she'd heard the rumors from her parents about the insanity that had happened at his house, but she wondered how much of it was actually true. There were signs of things that had been fixed, like the cabinet door and a new family portrait, but none of that meant that Randall had defended himself here against a multitude of dangerous assassins.

She almost interrupted to ask, wanting to dispel the rumors or give them weight, once and for all, but she didn't want to be rude. Maybe that was a tale for another day, too.

Teddy said to Randall, "Any chance you'd want to come out to Portland and sit in with our creative team?

We'd love to have you and of course, we'd compensate you for your time. Like a consultant. I was telling Sara that the guys we have now, they just want to talk about angles and percentages and wind speed. We need somebody like you to put meat on the bone."

Randall tilted his baseball cap higher on his head, crossed his arms, and said, "Hell, I don't know, man. I've had a rough few months lately. I'm kinda enjoying hanging out here and relaxing, you know?"

"I get it, I do, honestly. But *Sniper One*, it's gonna be huge. Bigger than huge. Your name will be on millions of phones around the world, rolling through the credits."

Sara could tell that Randall wasn't motivated by recognition and glory the way Teddy was. It showed in the way he smirked and readjusted his stance, the way he tried to stifle a chuckle.

"That's the problem," Randall said. "I still got too many people out there that don't like the look of my name. The only way they'd be happy to see it is if the damn thing showed up in the obituaries."

Teddy, not to be defeated, said, "Yeah, okay, but how about this... You come out to Portland for a week or two and share some details and after you're gone, we'll leak the story to the gaming community. Actually, yeah, that's perfect! We'll tell them we had an anonymous source—a former Marine Corps sniper that didn't want to be identified, who gave us all these top secret details. I mean, they wouldn't be *real* top-secret details, but you get what I'm saying. They'll eat it up."

"Still seems kinda risky to me, chief. You got a reporter that's nosey enough, he'll find a way to figure it out. After the year I've had, man, it's probably best for me to lay low."

Teddy nodded as he listened. He put a finger up to his mouth. The thinker.

Randall continued, "And besides, on the surface, being a sniper sounds like some cool shit, but in reality, it's all a lot of dressing up like a pile of leaves and waiting a week to pull the trigger."

The floorboard creaked under Sara's feet as she shifted to get comfortable. From all the research she'd done as the marketing director for LightPulse Productions, in order to promote their *Juggernaut* series, she knew that Randall was merely trying to downplay the reality.

She'd interviewed some former snipers herself. Read books by the greats like Carlos Hathcock and Chris Kyle. There were amazing stories of survival, dedication, and willpower that served to ensure a mission's success. Life as a sniper was more than being patient and pulling a trigger, she knew that for certain, and for Randall to seem so humble about it made her like and appreciate him even more.

Here was a former soldier that had served his country and done his duty like it was the natural order of things—not some blowhard who wanted to prove to the world what kind of chest-pounding, barbaric man he was.

Once Randall finished trying to convince Teddy that it was no big deal, Teddy took a step closer to him and said, "How does a hundred thousand dollars sound for a week of your time?"

"Teddy," Sara said, "don't badger the poor guy. Come on."

Randall smiled at her. "No worries, ma'am. Now I'm interested."

Teddy couldn't hide his excitement. "Interested enough, or should we talk about a higher number?"

"Let me think about it, okay?"

That appeared to be enough for Teddy—who reacted as if he'd gotten a solid confirmation—as he slapped his hands together then pumped his fist in the air.

Randall laughed. Sara shook her head.

"Hold your horses, chief. I'm not on an airplane just yet. How long are you in town?"

"Another three or four days as long as Sara doesn't kick me out."

Randall turned to her with one eyebrow arched.

"It's a long story," she said.

Teddy's phone buzzed on his hip. He checked the caller ID. "That's Irina. Hang on one sec, okay? Excuse me." He went across the kitchen, between Randall and Sara, then out the screen door. It slammed behind him, a clanging metal on metal noise that hurt Sara's ears.

She turned to Randall. "Thanks for humoring him."

"You used to work with him?"

"For years."

"And how in the hell did you handle that on a daily basis?" Randall was smiling as he asked. Not malicious, but exasperated.

"I know he's a bit overbearing, but that little munchkin's got a good heart. Well, *now* at least. It took me a long time to get him there."

"You two got history together?"

"We do, but not that kind. It's a story for another day."

Randall snorted and shrugged. "Right. I got plenty of those myself. Can I get you a beer? More coffee?" He moved over to the ancient refrigerator and pulled out a bottle of Budweiser.

After living in the Pacific Northwest fc
where craft brews flowed like river water, it   ⌐st
foreign to see a domestic beer. "No, thanks," she said.
"Where I come from, what you're holding is like a
bottle of Evian."

Randall popped the beer cap off the bottle.
"Sounds about right. Old habits. So I heard you were
from Oregon. What in the hell are you doing over
here?"

"Originally from northern Virginia, but how I got
out there and back here is an even longer story. We'll
have you and your family over one day for dinner. It'd
be good to get to know each other."

*And for me to find out how willing you'd be to shoot a
terrorist if she showed up here*, Sara thought.

"Absolutely."

Teddy flung open the screen door and said to Sara,
"We should head back."

"Why?" she asked. "What's wrong?"

"Irina said they're starting the press conference
early. Something about some new information that's
got everyone freaking out."

"What press conference?" Randall asked.

Sara eyed Teddy, almost telepathically asking him
if she should mention the details to Randall. What

were the consequences? Freak out the new neighbor or make an ally? Randall had seen some crazy stuff, she knew that much, so the likelihood of her story affecting him would be minimal. She hoped. On the other hand, she didn't want her first cordial meeting with Randall to be one where she begged for his help.

Teddy lifted one corner of his mouth and stepped through the door, allowing it to close quietly behind him.

Sara said, "How much time do we have?"

"Fifteen minutes."

Randall took another sip of beer. "Everything okay?"

"No, not exactly." Sara turned her eyes up to the ceiling and took a deep breath, preparing to take the risk. "I know this is going to sound ridiculous, but my folks—do you know the Thompsons?"

"Yeah, good people."

"They told me about your military background and I've been meaning to get over here and talk to you, but it never seemed like the right time and I didn't want to be rude and… You're going to think I belong up on the hill in the mental hospital."

"Ma'am, at some point, we all belong in a padded room."

***

Sara enjoyed the way Randall kept calling her 'ma'am' even though they were close to the same age. The southern hospitality and politeness around here was an added bonus she hadn't expected. But, what surprised her more was the way that Randall had immediately offered to help if she needed it.

Her story, and Teddy's story, would take too long to explain, so he'd walked back to her house with them in order to hear it all. Plus, he wanted to listen in on the press conference to get a better idea of what she was so afraid of. His wife, Alice, had begun homeschooling their boy Jesse, and the two of them were on an overnight retreat to Roanoke with the other moms and children, so he insisted he had some time to kill.

Along the way back to Sara's house, Teddy yammered about how brave they'd been in both situations, first Shelley, then Patty, as if it would impress the weathered veteran. Randall listened politely, and agreed that Teddy was most definitely a brave soul, and from what he'd heard, Sara *deserved* to be called a badass chick.

Once they'd returned to Sara's farmhouse, the three of them sat in the entertainment room while

SARA'S FEAR

Irina and Miss Willow took the children out back to
play in the large, open yard since the rain had passed
through.

Sara turned on the wall-mounted, flat screen
television and changed the channel from the Cartoon
Network over to CNN. They waited for a Cadillac
commercial to finish, then "Breaking News" soared
across the screen in white block letters against a blood
red background, accompanied by the familiar notes of
the CNN intro music and James Earl Jones' booming
voice.

"Let me ask you something," Randall said. He
moved over and sat down on the arm of the couch,
close to Sara. "What makes you think this prison break
has anything to do with these two women trying to kill
you?"

"If I told you all the details, we'd be here until next
Tuesday."

On the television, Wolf Blitzer walked toward a
massive screen behind him, pointing to a map of
Oregon. He said, "We're here with you live. More
coming out of Oregon as we're gearing up to listen to a
press conference that was moved up by an hour…"

Sara said, "The short version is, when we were
held hostage in Teddy's father's house, one of her
guys—"

"Guys?"

"Um…hitmen? Hired hands? I don't know what in the hell they're called, but I swear I heard him mention Shelley's name. I could've been imagining things or, you know, having some sort of traumatic flashback, but it stuck with me for some reason."

"What'd he say?"

"It wasn't to her and I only caught pieces of it, but it sounded like he said, '*Shelley, that girl in prison.*' It's not much, but believe me, the name catches my ear every time I hear it, no matter who it belongs to."

"Hmm."

"Hush," Teddy said, "here they come. Whoa, is that Barker?"

SIX

Patty sat in the window seat of the small, private jet. It hadn't been cheap, but the ability to maneuver around the U.S. unhindered made the extra zeroes worth it. Back before she'd failed to do away with Sara, and chose not to continue her mission by eliminating her target in France, it had been a close call getting into the States from Mexico, and she'd made better arrangements this time.

In the life of an international terrorist, haste meant the death penalty. The question now remained, was she going to take Shelley Sergeant with her afterward? A lot of that depended on how she behaved for the rest of this adventure.

She thought of it that way: an adventure. It wasn't a task, or a chore, or a game even, as Shelley kept calling it. Sure, it was fun, but this had become a quest. The pot of gold at the end of the rainbow. Finding El Dorado, the lost city of gold. Unearthing Blackbeard's treasure.

Except this time, watching Sara Winthrop die was the ultimate prize, more valuable than money, and more rewarding.

Patty daydreamed about how she would do it while Shelley slept in the seat across the aisle. When the young woman stirred and rolled her head to the side, Patty glanced over and took a longer look at her face. Patty had forced her to remove the eye patch before they'd gotten on the plane. Surely, in a day or two, the pilots would recognize her on television as one of the women they'd flown across the country. The eye patch would be unmistakable. One of them would alert the local authorities and they'd know where to focus their efforts.

Maybe it wouldn't ruin the adventure totally, but it would definitely hinder her plans.

She examined Shelley's face closely, remembering what she'd seen of the poor girl back at Coffee Creek when she'd visited with Quirk. The gnarled, mottled skin. The purple-scarred rivulets along her cheek. The thin strip of discoloration that formed a ring around her neck. All signs of an attempt on Shelley's life. The prisoners, plenty of them mothers themselves, hadn't taken kindly to the new inmate who'd nearly succeeded in murdering Sara's children to achieve her objective.

Where they had seen a horrible, disgusting human being and tried to send her back to Hell, Patty saw the beauty in Shelley's angry and vengeful plans. She'd tried, and failed, to gouge out Sara Winthrop's heart, hitting her in the place where she knew it would hurt the most. Patty admired the effort, but scoffed at the poor execution.

She leaned closer to Shelley's face and stared at the lumpy folds where the eye had once been. They were a mixture of light pink and flesh tones. Hills and valleys where the stitches had pulled and prevented a proper healing.

Patty thought, *Maybe she should've left the eye patch on. That mess is just as obvious.*

Memorable, for certain, but would the pilots make the connection?

Possibly, though if her plans went as she expected, they'd be gone by the time either the pilot or co-pilot had seen enough to identify her. They'd land in Bristol, at Tri-Cities Regional Airport, and then they'd be gone. She already had a car waiting in the long-term lot—all they had to do was drive away.

At best, the pilots could say that Shelley's last known location was on the tarmac of TRI.

The pilot, a man named Jeff, came over the intercom and said, "Miss Wilson, we're about to begin our descent into northeast Tennessee where the temperature is a cozy sixty-one degrees with overcast skies. We could hit some turbulence, so I'd like to ask that you and your guest please return to your seats and buckle up."

The co-pilot, Smiling Dave, as he'd informed them, poked his head out of the cabin, smiling, and said, "Let us know if you need anything, and thanks for the company!"

Patty wanted to punch him on principle.

Smiling Dave waved one last time and closed the cabin door.

Beside her, Shelley moaned, stretched, and opened her eye. "What'd he say? Are we there already?"

"You've been out since we hit altitude right out of Minneapolis."

Shelley sat up and took a drink from her water bottle. "I haven't slept like that since…damn, since the night I put a bullet in Sara's husband."

"That relaxing, huh?" Patty knew what Shelley meant. She'd experienced the same feeling of satisfaction before with Sara's former classmates as each one of them evaporated in the explosion of Quirk's handiwork.

"I slept like the dead that night. No pun intended." Shelley arched her back and reached up to her missing left eye. She rubbed at the skin and felt around her forehead, then on top of her head. "Oh, yeah. Forgot."

Patty couldn't recall the last time she'd felt anything resembling sympathy, but a flicker of it traipsed through her mind as she watched Shelley turn her face away. "You can put your eye patch back on once we're away from those two." She wanted to sound reassuring, maybe even a little bit human, because that still existed somewhere inside her psyche, but the statement came out sounding more like a mother telling her child that she could have her toy back once the chores were finished.

"No," Shelley said. "I'm done hiding it. I want her to see. I want her to know I earned it."

Her. Sara. A tingle of excitement skittered across Patty's skin. Maybe Shelley Sergeant had been a good choice after all. "Good. Hold onto that fire."

The small jet bounced and rattled, then dipped when it hit an empty air pocket. Shelley yelped and flung a hand across the aisle, grabbing Patty's wrist for comfort. "God, I hate flying," she said.

Another tingle emerged in Patty, in a place she hadn't foreseen, and she allowed Shelley's hand to linger for a moment. She'd been with women before, but she'd never preferred their company. Each and every time it had been to complete an assignment for someone with deep pockets and a list of enemies. To get close enough to the drug lord in Caracas,

Venezuela, she'd made love to his wife while he watched, sipping wine and smoking marijuana. She'd eliminated them both the second he tried to climb into bed.

Next had been the brilliant programmer in Barcelona, Spain. She'd hired a prostitute for show, seduced the squirrely nerd in a bar, and then killed them both on a balcony overlooking the tree-lined street of *La Rambla*.

There were others, but they weren't nearly as memorable or exciting. There was something alluring about the thrill of being nude and vulnerable in the minutes before purging a mark. It wasn't as exhilarating as her desire to be caught in the act, but it was fun nonetheless.

She'd never been mentally attracted to any of the women she'd been with. It was all part of the job, so the fact that she'd felt something with Shelley's touch was both tantalizing and surprising. Back in the Explorer, she'd been ready to slam the young woman's face into the dashboard to make a point.

But this? What was this? Desire?

And why? Was it because Shelley was damaged too? Was there some underlying connection, some universal bond between them?

That pure moment of "Hey, you're just like me,

and it's us against the world," was that what it was?

Regardless, there was no room for it. Lust and attraction, emotion, they caused problems.

Patty yanked her arm away. She said, "Touch me again and I *will* cut you." The threat was empty, made more as a reassurance to herself than a warning to Shelley.

"Jesus. Whatever." Shelley pulled her arm back across the aisle. "I told you, flying freaks me out."

"There are plenty of things you should be more afraid of."

"Like what? The infamous Patty Kellog?"

"And then some."

"Uh-huh." Shelley shook her head, scoffed, and pulled a small bottle of vodka from the cabinet along the cabin wall. She twisted the cap, gulped down the contents, and reached for another. She poured the next one over a cup of ice and sat with it in her lap, sipping occasionally. "Sorry. I'm fine... I get nervous when we start bouncing around like that." As if on cue, the plane dipped, shook, and rattled some of the items in the overhead bin.

Jeff informed them over the intercom that everything was fine, but they'd need to remain seated and buckled for the duration of the trip.

Smiling Dave opened the cockpit door, smiled,

and said, "Wheels down in fifteen minutes!"

He closed the door and Shelley said, "I'd like to punch him on principle."

"No shit," Patty agreed. Then, sensing that might have been a positive affirmation to the impetuous apprentice, she added, "But don't. They live. No questions."

Shelley replied, "They've seen my face…or what's left of it."

"My way or no way, remember? Too many bodies leaves a trail. It attracts attention. In fact, dead bodies attract more attention than a couple of pilots who may or *may not* make the connection if they happen to see your face on the Post Office wall a month from now. Even if these guys watch the news—even if your face is all over it, they can call in a tip, but we'll be so far gone by then that it won't make a difference."

"But—"

Patty lowered her voice and leaned across the aisle. Shifting tones now, she morphed from the den mother that snipped at heels and ears to keep young pups in line to the calm, soothing confidante that confided and consoled. Why? She didn't know, exactly. Something inside her suggested that this girl would respond better to a comforting figure, rather than a heavy hand and vitriolic reprimands. "Relax. I know you're...what...what are you? Eager? Green? Still wet behind the ears? Listen, you've got potential. Amazing potential. You remind me of myself when I was your age. I was too impulsive and ready to get back at everyone, you know? I didn't care how it happened, because all I wanted was to give the whole world a sledgehammer to the side of its head.

"It didn't take me long to figure out that doing things that way led to too many unwanted consequences. I learned to plan, to take my time, to think through my methods. Every day is a learning experience. Slitting a throat one way is preferable to another. Shoot a guy in the right spot, he doesn't bleed on the carpet so much. Whatever, you know? But you take it slow. Be methodical. Think, think, and think some more. I've been doing this for twenty years, and there are people out there, like this guy I know called The Spirit, who still acts like I'm a bull in a china shop. They say my methods are too reckless and rash, even after I've planned and it's taken six months to complete a job. Is any of this making sense to you?"

Shelley nodded and took a sip of her vodka. "I guess. You're telling me to put on my big girl panties."

Patty tucked a loose strand of hair behind Shelley's ear. "Right. Exactly. Now do me a favor and try not to kill everything that looks at you sideways. You stick with me, you listen to me, you'll learn from me. I'll teach you how to feed that nastiness that you're carrying around inside and how to earn more money than you'll ever need in five lifetimes."

"It's not about the money."

"It will be once I introduce you to the right crowd."

"So, it's like, murder for fun and profit?"

"More or less. But it's a lot more than that. You get to travel around the world, meet interesting people, then kill them. Trust me, it does more good for that damaged brain in your head than years of sitting in a psychiatrist's office. Been there, done that, watched him bleed out on a sunny Thursday afternoon. Best decision I ever made."

"They had an in-house shrink back at the prison. The guy's name was Pederson. Had bad teeth, bad hair. Smelled like he always had dog shit on the bottom of his shoes. I hated him. Hated him," Shelley said, turning her head upward for emphasis. "After he put his hand down my jumpsuit the second time, I had him on the ground with my knee in his balls and a pen held up to his jugular. He didn't do it again."

"Why didn't you do it?"

"They were serving macaroni at lunch and I didn't want to miss out."

Patty chuckled. "Good girl. That's what I'm talking about. Sacrifices for the sake of getting the job done correctly. It wasn't the right time and you recognized it. Show me more of that and maybe one of these days we'll pay Pederson a visit."

Shelley drained the last of her vodka. Glassy-eyed, she propped her chin up on her hand. "Got it, boss. So what's the plan with that whore Sara, huh? Are you gonna give me a chance to play the game?"

SEVEN

Sara turned up the television's volume.

Teddy asked, "Why would Barker be there? Dude looks like they dragged him out of his hospital bed."

She shushed him as Randall got up and moved around her, sat on the couch, then leaned forward to listen.

Wolf Blitzer's voice came from off camera, saying, *"We should be getting started any second now. I'm going to sit back and listen with you all as we're about to learn more details from this tragic event."*

All three watched as a man stepped up to the podium, in front of Barker, but behind the collection of microphones that sported various news channel insignias. He wore a navy blue suit with a white collared shirt underneath, accompanied by a red power tie. He had a shaved head and a standard-issue mustache resting on his upper lip that paled in comparison to Barker's. The man removed a folded sheet of paper from inside his suit jacket, cleared his throat, and donned a pair of reading glasses.

Sara wanted to scream at him, whoever he was, and tell him to hurry up. Her insides were wobbly and the burn in her lungs made it difficult to breathe. With any luck, they would report that the inmates had been captured and that Shelley Sergeant was never one of the four.

However, the presence of Barker was not a good sign. Why was he involved?

The man at the podium coughed into his fist and said, "Good afternoon, I am Agent Grady Morrow with the Federal Bureau of Investigation. Please hold all your questions until I have completed my statement and then we will open it up to further discussion. First, our hearts go out to the families of the two men slain during this event. Prison guards Warren Barnes and Donny Potter died at the scene and we mourn this tragic loss of life with their families." Morrow's voice was solemn and robotic. Sara thought it wouldn't be terribly comforting to hear those words if she'd been part of the families who'd lost loved ones.

Morrow continued, "At approximately four a.m. this morning, what appeared to be a paramilitary group of two males and one female assaulted Coffee Creek Correctional Facility. Initially these reports were denied by the warden and local law enforcement in an effort to contain informational leaks, but in conjunction with the FBI's involvement, video surveillance and further circumstances have proven this to be true. At this time, no known organization has claimed responsibility, nor do we believe it to be the work of a known terrorist group, foreign or domestic."

He cleared his throat again. The sound frayed Sara's nerves even more.

Agent Morrow continued, "This was a highly trained group of individuals and we are pursuing with intent to capture to the fullest extent of our capabilities. After superior cooperative efforts by prison officials and local law enforcement, we have determined that four inmates escaped and as of thirty minutes ago, three of them were captured ten miles from the prison. At this time, their names are being withheld."

Teddy squeezed Sara's shoulder. "Sweet! They got three of them. That's awesome, huh?"

She managed a grin. "Yeah, so far, so good."

Agent Morrow was still reading. "And due to the correctional facility's video surveillance, we have reason to believe that the inmate who remains at large is with this paramilitary group."

"Damn," Randall said. "They've got some balls to break *into* prison."

"At present, we ask that you remain cautious and aware of any suspicious activity involving two men and two women, believed to be driving a mid-1990s blue Ford Explorer with Oregon license plates. While no details are known regarding the assailants, the escaped inmate's photo has been released to all media outlets and should be appearing on your screen soon. The missing individual is Shelley Ann Sergeant, approximately five feet, four inches tall, one hundred and fifteen pounds, with blonde hair, and also known to wear an eye patch to hide injuries sustained in a prison attack two years prior."

Sara had already gotten up and moved close to the television, one arm around her ribs and a hand covering her mouth. She couldn't stand still. Her legs were rubber; knees shaky and weak. When Shelley's disfigured face flashed up on the screen, scarred and mangled with one eye covered by the black eye patch, Sara crumbled to the floor.

"I am in charge of this investigation and we will be treating this as a full-scale fugitive manhunt. I am assisted by Detective Emerson Barker of the Portland Police Department who volunteered as part of this special assignment and we can assure you that we will do everything possible to ensure your safety. If you have any information regarding the whereabouts of these individuals, call the hotline listed on your screen. We have agents standing by to take your calls and will follow all viable leads. Again, our heartfelt condolences to the families of Warren Barnes and Donny Potter.

This concludes our prepared statement and we have time left for a couple of questions."

Sara shivered and pulled her knees closer to her chest.

Were she and her children, and Miss Willow, far enough away? How far was far enough?

She thought back to that day in Jim Rutherford's house. She thought about Patty Kellog and the men that were with her. All highly trained, but taken by surprise with Teddy's quick action and Vadim Bariskov's betrayal. Patty's body was not amongst the dead when they searched the house.

Was it possible that she was part of the group that attacked Coffee Creek?

God, that would be so insane. But is it possible?

While a reporter asked an innocuous question about timing and standard FBI practices, Teddy lowered himself onto the floor and scooted over next to Sara. He put his arm around her and said, "Don't worry, okay? They're three thousand miles away. She won't make it very far."

Sara fought the urge to throw up. "Teddy?"

"Huh?"

"What if it was Patty? You know, that helped her escape."

"What? *Pffft.* Not a chance. She probably crawled

off into a hole and died somewhere after Dad's house blew up."

Randall asked, "Patty's the one you were telling me about, right?"

Sara nodded.

On the television, a reporter stood up and asked, "Agent Morrow, about ten minutes before the press conference began, we received reports of a murdered couple found in the Cascades. Do you think that's in any way related?"

"We are pursuing all relevant leads."

"But do you think it's related?"

"As I said, we're pursuing all relevant leads. We will follow up with another press conference as soon as we have pertinent information to share. Thank you for your time."

Sara reached up and turned the television off. The screen went black.

Randall said, "So what're you thinking? That was every bit of the bad news you were expecting, right?"

Sara nodded. Teddy shrugged.

Randall got up from the couch and walked around the coffee table. He was quiet when he moved, perhaps from years of creeping stealthily through jungles and across deserts, sneaking up on his prey.

Sara watched as he stood at the large picture

window that overlooked the farm, the dilapidated barn with faded gray wood and a rusted tin roof, and the green hills beyond, scanning the open land. He pushed a curtain to the side and said, "I'm inclined to agree with Mr. Rutherford here. They're three thousand miles away and if you've ever watched any of these fugitive pursuits unfold on the nightly news, about a week from now, some big group of trigger happy feds will corner these guys in a cabin in the middle of a forest in northern California. They'll toss in a few smoke bombs, accidentally set the place on fire, and then all that's left will be a pile of toasted dipshits."

"Are you sure?"

Randall crossed his arms and shook his head. "I learned a long time ago that it's not a good idea to make guarantees. Too many variables. But more often than not, that's what happens. My guess is, your friend Shelley and this group of chowderheads will make a mistake somewhere along the way. They'll do something dumb in a gas station and the next thing you know, we're watching a live feed from a couple of different helicopters. Now, my question is, if these three folks broke into prison to get this girl out, what was their reason? Who is she? Is she important? Got money?"

"Not really." Sara pushed herself up from the

floor, extended a hand to Teddy, and helped him to his feet. She walked over to the wet bar and poured herself a small scotch in a glass tumbler. And, for good measure, she poured two more for Teddy and Randall. He joined them and they stood, sipping in silence until Sara said, "Like I said earlier, she was just this brilliant young woman that came to work for me at LightPulse. My husband had left me for her and when he wanted to leave and come back to his family, she murdered him then kidnapped my kids to get back at me."

"Get back at *you*?"

"Yeah. She was jealous. And her brother almost beat Teddy into a pile of mush, too. Anyway, that's such a long story and I really don't want to talk about it. What I'm trying to say is, I have no idea if she had money to pay someone to break her out or what. The only thing I can think of is what I'd said about one of Patty Kellog's goons maybe, possibly, mentioning Shelley's name. Why? I don't know. God, I don't know anything." She downed the last of her scotch and reached for the bottle again.

"Tell me again who this Kellog woman is? I've got some connections to her kind. Maybe I've heard of her."

"Short version or long version?"

Randall checked his watch. "Alice and my boy

won't be back until tomorrow, and you still got plenty of scotch left in that bottle."

Sara smiled. It was strained, but genuine. "Okay, long version." She freshened his glass, along with Teddy's, and told the story of Patty Kellog. Hinting at some parts and elaborating on others. Patty Kellog was dangerous. She was unstable. She was the former leader of a small terrorist group known as The Clan. They blew people up.

And, apparently, Patty Kellog was able to cheat death, or she only had eight of her nine lives remaining.

"If there's a connection between her and Shelley Sergeant, I have no idea what it could be. The story was all over the newspapers a couple of years ago. It's possible that Patty saw something and decided she could use a new partner."

Randall said, "Anything's possible. Y'all mentioned a security system on the way up here. What've you got?"

"Would you like to see it?"

"Of course. If I'm gonna help keep an eye on your place, it'd be nice to know what you've got already. There's stuff down there at the house that might do you some good, but if you've already got a whole system installed, I doubt my two-by-fours to nail over your windows could top it."

Teddy asked, "You've got guns, don't you?"

"That I do, T-bird. That I do. Have you shot much before?"

"Enough to know what I'm doing." Teddy winked at Sara. "You hear that? He called me T-bird."

"So that's better than Little One?"

"What do you think?" To Randall, he added, "I'm a pretty good shot. Sara can tell you."

"Every little bit helps. And speaking of that… Sara, you want me to call my sister-in-law to come have a look, too? Mary runs her own P.I. business over in town. She does good work, even though I joke around that all she does is try to figure out who's giving the mayor a little pickle tickle in the back of his BMW."

Sara was one shortened breath away from a minor panic attack, but the scotch had done some good, and it felt good to chuckle slightly at Randall's crude attempt at humor. "I knew that, actually. My folks mentioned her a while back, and yeah, if you think she's got the time." Sara caught herself. She was still getting used to the fact that she'd be able to *buy* someone's time, if it were necessary. The millions weren't going to spend themselves, and what better use than to add an extra layer of protection for her family?

"You know, why don't you give her a call? Let her know that I'd like to hire her. I'll make her trip worth it."

EIGHT

When the Learjet landed near Bristol, Tennessee at the Tri-Cities Regional Airport and taxied to the private hangars, Patty made sure to have Shelley depart the plane first in order to keep a careful watch on her. Jeff and his co-pilot Smiling Dave stood side-by-side near the exit, and Patty hoped to prevent their harm if Shelley got jumpy.

Smiling Dave smiled and tipped an imaginary hat as Jeff said, "Thanks for flying with us today. I hope it was a pleasant one."

Shelley was tipsy from the vodka, and when she reached with a hand toward the pilot's face, Patty tensed. Instead of clawing at his eyes, Shelley patted his cheek, said thanks, then made her way down the exit stairs.

Patty nodded to them both.

"Can we help you with your luggage?" Smiling Dave asked.

"No, I got it."

"We'll be making a return trip with two more clients tomorrow morning if you're looking for a ride back. We can speak to them about splitting the costs if you're interested."

"That won't be necessary, but thank you."

"Any time you need us, ma'am, we're only a hop, skip, and short flight away."

"Good, thank you, again." *Now stop talking to me, idiot.* Patty didn't want to be rude—rude meant memorable—but she also didn't want to stand around gabbing with two individuals who might easily identify her and Shelley. Was it too late to worry about that? Did it matter? Not if her preparations stayed intact. "Which way to the terminal? We're meeting family there." She had lied, hoping to further distract the pilots from her true intent.

Jeff leaned his head out the fuselage door and pointed. "Just over there. Tri-Cities is about the size of a Wal-Mart, so I doubt you'll get lost."

Patty feigned interest, thanked them again, then descended to the tarmac where Shelley stood, wobbly from the alcohol, looking bewildered. Patty said, "What's wrong?"

"Nothing, it's just—"

"Good, then walk. Now. Quickly. Quickly. Tell me on the way."

They shuffled across the tarmac, Patty urging her to walk at a brisk pace but nothing out of the ordinary.

Shelley said, "It's weird, you know?"

"What is?"

"It's weird how you can get into this big metal tube, then you sit down and take a nap, then when you wake up, it's like you're in a different world."

"You're drunk."

"No, I'm serious." She slurred the 'serious,' further confirming Patty's assessment. "It's such a different experience from driving. When you drive somewhere, you get to see all the changes going on around you as it happens, but when you fly, it's almost like you're in a teleporter that takes a really long time."

Patty gripped Shelley's arm tighter, leading her into the Tri-Cities terminal, up the stairs, and into the lobby. They stopped long enough to purchase a large bottle of water, some ibuprofen, and a cup of coffee. In the small café, the news was playing on a flat-screen television hanging above the clerk. A man with a shaved head and a ridiculous mustache spoke in front of a herd of reporters. Behind him stood yet another man that she was quite familiar with: Detective Emerson Barker.

Patty glanced over and into the open, light-filled lobby. Shelley slumped in a gray chair in the waiting area. With her head flopped to the side, she'd already passed out again.

The clerk said, "That'll be twelve dollars and twenty-nine cents, please."

She handed over a twenty and tried to hear what the man on television was saying. "At approximately four a.m. this morning, what appeared to be a paramilitary group of two males and one female assaulted Coffee Creek Correctional Facility."

Patty cursed to herself, took her change, and moved toward her new...what was Shelley? Employee? Henchwoman? Crony? She patted her on the cheek. "Up, up. Let's go."

Shelley snorted when she opened her eyes and groggily poured herself out of the chair and into a standing position. "Should've known better. No drinks in prison means no tolerance means I'm all kinds of drunkie poo!" She giggled and fell into Patty.

"Get control of yourself, right now, you hear me? You're making a scene, and we don't *want* a scene. The FBI is already doing a press conference about your escape, so we need to keep our heads down, okay?"

Shelley giggled again. "Yes, mommy."

Thankfully, they made it to the long-term parking lot before Shelley ran for a trashcan and vomited into it. Once Patty had her successfully contained within the car, head lolling to the side and against the window, she forced two ibuprofen into Shelley's mouth, made her drink some water to swallow the pills, and then exited the lot, heading west for I-81 in the overcast, afternoon light of northeast Tennessee.

Patty exhaled heavily and felt her muscles release some of their tension. She was confident they'd made it out unnoticed.

Sara Winthrop's house and Patty's vengeance were only sixty miles away.

But first, they had one stop to make.

***

Patty took the exit ramp off I-81 and headed west, through the town of Abingdon, Virginia—a neat place from what she remembered. Back when she was a girl, maybe eight years old, they'd stopped here once to see a play at the Barter Theater. It was *The Wizard of Oz*, and she saw it in her mind's eye as if she was sitting in the balcony yesterday. The Wicked Witch's face was painted green. The tall pointy hat. That howling, cackling laughter. Back when she was pulling The Clan together, she debated using Wicked Witch as a codename, but had eventually decided on Boudica since the association with the Celtic queen's history suited her mission's objective better.

Now, as they drove past an area that had sprouted

considerably since she'd been there over thirty years ago, she tried to focus on the task ahead rather than what lay outside. It was nearly impossible. It'd changed so much. Shops and gas stations and fast food joints. Streetlights and so many cars. She had some pictures in her mind of what it used to be like, but apparently the town commission had contracted plenty of work to beautify the place. Restored buildings, colorful landscaping, and historical markers lined Highway 11.

She thought about how far she'd come since those days. She wasn't a little girl anymore. She was feared and respected—by some—all around the world, from London to Shanghai to Los Angeles. She'd gone from pigtails and lollipops to needles filled with poison and garrote wires.

Nostalgia? Forget it. Life didn't wait for those who dwelled in the past.

Although, seeing the Barter Theater again as she drove past brought back yet another flood of memories. Mother, Father, and Sis. Smiling and singing together in the car.

Dead now. Every one of them.

Acknowledge and move on.

Past Abingdon and further west, out into the country where the low hills and rolling farmland stretched for miles, she was able to clear her mind and think about what was to come next. She allowed Shelley to doze in the passenger's seat, head awkwardly propped against the window, as they passed mobile homes and well-kept barns. Cattle munched lazily in green fields. A shiny, black foal ran parallel to its mother, manes blowing in the wind.

She wished the blue sky would break through the clouds. Just because she was thirty miles away from murdering a small family didn't mean she couldn't appreciate the beauty of nature. A doctor doesn't ignore the glory of a morning sunrise because he has to be in surgery later that day. A CEO of a multi-national corporation wouldn't disregard the overwhelming magnificence of a Hawaii waterfall because he had an important meeting in a day or two.

Her line of work may have been inhuman, but it didn't mean that she wasn't human. Right?

Patty rolled down the window of the rented Honda and inhaled deeply. Fresh, clean earth with a hint of hay and other unrecognizable nature scents.

It'd been so long since she'd stopped to smell *life*. She couldn't remember the last time. Always running from one airport to the next, taking out marks in Sydney and Buenos Aires, jumping over to Venezuela and then Thailand and Russia. It was exhausting. She actually missed being able to breathe without an elevated heart rate.

Okay, maybe the nostalgia thing wasn't so bad. Maybe after she took care of Sara Winthrop and figured out what to do with Shelley, she'd take a vacation. She deserved one.

But not here. She had a feeling that her time in the U.S. would be limited after the screwed up mess at Coffee Creek and what would happen within twenty-four hours at the Winthrop farm only a few miles north of here. With all of its technological advancements, the FBI, along with its cooperation with other government entities, had gotten so much better in recent years. Much more adept than some of the foreign countries she worked in where innocence could be purchased rather than proven.

She found the highway marker she was looking for, turned left, and felt the gravel vibrating the car as the tires rolled along the unpaved road.

Shelley groaned and lifted her head. "Where are we?"

"Southwest Virginia."

"You sure? Looks like they filmed *Hee-Haw* here."

"How's your head?"

"It feels like someone is beating me with a mallet. Where'd those ibuprofen go?"

Patty opened the center console and tossed the bottle to Shelley. "Water's down there at your feet."

Shelley popped the top, poured a number of gel capsules into her mouth, then washed them down. "Where we going?"

"To see some friends."

Shelley scoffed. "You have friends? Are they, like, real friends, or *friends* in quotation marks?"

"You'll see when we get there."

"Oh, such mystery." Shelley reached over and turned the radio on, flipping from channel to channel. "Country... Country... Gospel... Oh, hey, here's a country channel. Imagine that." She slapped the dial and the music went silent.

"How old are you?" Patty asked. She was genuinely inquiring, but the fact that Shelley was behaving like an impatient, bored teenager made her even more curious.

"Why? Am I annoying you, Mommy?"

Patty scowled as she shook her head. At the next open spot on the roadside, she whipped the steering wheel to the right and skidded to a halt. Gravel kicked up and rattled under the car. Though it'd been drizzling recently, the tires dug low enough to reach dry dirt, sending up a small plume of dust that the breeze carried away.

"Jesus, you do know my head is pounding, don't you?" Shelley said, holding her temples. "What did I do now?"

"One last time, Shelley. If you're going to be a professional, start acting like it. I'm sick of this shit already. I don't want to baby you and I don't want to mother you, but from what I learned, you were getting close to being a respectable badass before you went to prison. That shit you pulled with Sara? That game? Putting her kids in the boxes? That was some serious evil genius stuff—I want *that* Shelley back. Look, I don't know what happened in prison...

"Maybe they did some damage to your emotional *whatever*, maybe somebody made you her girlfriend, maybe you had to hide in the corner to stay alive. Whatever it was, you went backwards. You're not a child. You're not some...some silly teenager any more. You were a strong, powerful woman. I see myself in you, okay? Now that there are two of us, we'll be unstoppable, but I need you to find the real Shelley again, and I need you to do it right now, because the people we're going to see—they will slit our throats if you so much as stick out your tongue. No more of this teenage angst bullshit. Grow up. Be that *woman* again."

"Are you finished?"

"Yes."

"Thank you."

"For what?"

"My freedom. Seriously. Or whatever this is," Shelley said, motioning around the car, pointing out toward the fields. "But understand one thing—yes, you saved me, you rode in on your black horse and rescued me like a pretty little damsel in distress, or some princess up in a tower, but know this, you crazy bitch, you *do not* own me. You will never *own* me. I am dangerous, *so* dangerous, and this act you've got going on where you think I'm some little birdie under your wing…shove it up your ass. *You don't own me.* I don't owe you anything. I was fine where I was and I'm still here because I *want* to be here, and so help me God, if you ever try to pull any of that mommy shit on me again, I will eat your throat and drink your blood. Are we clear?"

Patty smiled and softly said, "There's the fire. There's the woman I want." She grabbed Shelley by the back of the head, drew her in close and mashed their lips together. She was thrilled when Shelley didn't pull away.

NINE

Sara sat at the kitchen table with Randall Blevins, drinking coffee, and holding the mug tightly in an effort to keep her hands steady. Miss Willow had coaxed Lacey, Callie, and Jacob inside, and the four of them were down in the basement watching a movie in the theater room. She'd had it installed weeks ago, and though she loathed to use it as a babysitter, the modified room with stadium seating and a projector hanging above, displaying the movie on nearly an entire wall, was a perfect place for the kids to escape when she needed some of her own downtime.

Teddy and Irina had gone for a hike in the hills behind Sara's farmhouse. She'd protested, slightly, but with Teddy's usual annoying insistence and Randall's assurance that they were safe in the woods, she'd relented. Teddy had said, "I don't know about you, but I can't sit there and twiddle my thumbs, waiting for some news. It'll drive me bonkers."

She'd made the argument that having a mild sense of cabin fever was better than death, because who knew what Patty Kellog could've set in motion already.

Before he'd walked out the door, Teddy added,

"Sara, come on, dude. I honestly don't believe that
Patty Kellog would be involved. That old KGB guy
that was with me said she was an international terrorist.
Why in the hell would she waste her time with some
bush league criminal in prison? *Does not compute.* It'll be
fine. Randall says so, don't you, Randall?"

Randall had nodded, and as she'd watched them
walk across the back porch, the wood creaking beneath
their feet, she'd hoped to God he was right.

If he wasn't, the answer was obvious. There were
only two people in the world that held murderous
grudges against her, and one had the resources to
break the other one out of prison, simple as that.

Sara sipped her coffee while Randall read over the
schematics and instructional guides associated with the
home's security system. They were waiting on Randall's
sister-in-law, Mary Walker, to arrive. Sara checked the
wall clock—an old-fashioned cuckoo that Miss Willow
had gotten Sara for her birthday—and saw that they
had another fifteen minutes before Mary would arrive.
As Randall read, Sara decided that fifteen minutes of
silence wouldn't be possible. She was too worried,
fearful, and wired from so much coffee.

"Randall?"

"Mmm?" He looked up from the blueprints where he'd been noting the locations of cameras and motion detectors.

"Did I thank you yet?"

"Yes, ma'am, and I've already lost track of how many times."

"You don't have to do this, you know. I mean, I just walked into your house and said, 'Hey, nice to meet you, wanna come help me keep an eye out for terrorists?' It was rude and presumptuous and...and I don't even have enough shitty adjectives for what it is. It's wrong and I shouldn't have done it. I shouldn't have dragged you into this."

"You sure didn't have to twist my arm an awful lot." Randall pushed the blueprints to the side and propped himself up at the elbows. "I did this for a living. I saw things you wouldn't believe out there in the jungles. I worked with, and *killed*, men that make you wake up sweating in the middle of the night. I hate to say it, because I don't want to make light of your situation, but this is small taters. Ain't no big deal, not at all, and besides...well, I wasn't a hundred percent honest with you, either."

"You weren't?"

Randall readjusted his baseball cap. Sara had noticed it was a habit of his whenever he was about to saw something he wasn't comfortable with. "Do me a favor and don't mention this to your folks, because I promised 'em I wouldn't say a doggone word…"

"My parents?"

Randall looked to his left, then his right, saying, "I, um, I already knew about part of your situation. Most of it, if you wanna know the truth. Ran into them a while back, not long after you moved to town, and we had breakfast together over at the Corner Café, the one there on Main Street. Anyway, long story short, they asked me if I'd keep watch around your property, you know, just to make sure there wasn't something funky going on over here."

"Why didn't you say something? Why didn't they?"

"I reckon they didn't want you to think they were butting in on your life."

"They're my parents for God's sake. That's what parents do."

"Look, your mom and pop were thinking more on the lines of a guardian angel. It wasn't a big deal. Hasn't been. A fella's gotta sleep now and again, but whenever I'm home, I make sure to peek over."

Sara didn't know how to feel. Thankful, in a sense, for the fact that there had been an extra set of eyes out there, competent ones, keeping her under loose surveillance. Yet, it was almost disconcerting knowing that if Randall had been doing it this whole time, and she'd been unaware, who else could be watching? She'd been so careful, but now, paranoia seemed like a valid emotion.

"I'm sorry," Randall said. "We probably should've said something."

"I can't believe you knew. That's why you were readjusting your hat so much. You were uncomfortable."

Randall grinned and leaned back in the chair. "What was I doing?"

"You mess with your hat whenever you're uncomfortable or feeling awkward."

"No shit?"

Sara broke eye contact and stared into her mug. "Yeah, it's probably a little weird that I noticed something like that, but after working for LightPulse for so many years, I pay more attention to people. We were always trying to give our characters a sense of realism, so we'd add in these movements and character quirks to make them more human. You said Jesse plays *Juggernaut*, right?"

"Plays it more than he breathes, I think."

"Have you seen much of it, like the cutaway scenes? The ones where it looks like you're watching a movie?"

"Yeah."

"There's one scene in the game where General Cragg is constantly tugging on his left earlobe. We wrote that into the game because Teddy's father, Jim, the owner, used to do that all the freakin' time. It was like his poker tell for when he was thinking something over." She couldn't be sure if Randall gave two hoots about the minor details of a video game, but it was a relief to talk about something she was familiar with.

Work. That old security blanket. The place she could hide when the fearful thoughts in her mind drifted to dark places. Taking the time off and relaxing here in Virginia, supposedly hidden, or with a low profile at the least, had been both a blessing and a curse. The downtime spent relaxing on the front porch, rocking back and forth, watching nature go by, had been invaluable. She could breath again without getting lightheaded.

On the other hand, when her parents were away, the kids were in school, and Miss Willow was out with her quilting committee, it offered too many opportunities for her thoughts to grow cloudy and fearful, wondering if she'd make the right choice by bringing her family here.

Still, the distance between her and her past had grown both physically and over time, which was more acceptable than allowing the horrible memories to soak her life like the rains of Portland she'd left behind.

"Anyway," she said. "That's all. If you play poker, you might want to take your hat off."

"Son of a gun. I wondered how those shitheads in my unit could always tell when I was bluffing." He shook his head wistfully. "All these years. I haven't touched a deck of cards in twenty years because I just thought I sucked at it."

Sara jumped when a buzzer sounded on the wall. Someone was calling up from the front gate.

"Easy," Randall said, getting up from the table. "That'd be Mary."

"How do you know?"

Randall tapped his ear. "I know what her car sounds like."

"Really?" Sara stood up, wiping her sweaty palms on her thin jacket. "They all sound the same to me."

"You go over to town, yeah, it's nothing but a rumbling of engines and tires, but out here in the sticks, it's different. You learn after a while that each sound has it's own...shit, I don't know... It's own reality, I reckon. You hear, you listen, you learn."

"Good to know," Sara said. She stepped around his massive frame—he smelled like sweet laundry detergent, which was out of place for such a gruff country-boy—and spoke with Mary through the intercom.

Moments later, Sara opened the front door and for a second, a small measure of panic rippled through her stomach. She'd been expecting someone that partially resembled Randall's wife, Alice, who was also Mary's sister. She hadn't spent too much time with her, but where Alice was taller, with bottle-blonde hair, a fake tan, and blue eyes, the woman at her doorstep was entirely different. A thick mop of wavy brunette hair, about Teddy's height with dark brown eyes, and naturally brown tones to her skin. She was pretty with a warm smile. She also leaned on a hand-carved, wooden cane.

When the woman extended her hand to introduce herself, Sara caught a glimpse of a concealed weapon inside of a leather shoulder holster.

"I'm Mary Walker. You must be Sara."

"I am." Sara's eyes remained fixated on the spot where she'd seen the firearm.

Mary must have noticed. "I can take it off if you'd like. Randall says you have kids around."

"No, no, sorry." Sara waved her in. "That was

106

rude of me. I didn't mean—"

Mary chuckled as she shook Sara's hand. "Hey, no, don't worry about it. I know guns can freak people out. I'd wear it around my ankle, but I've already got a smaller one down there and two is just bad fashion."

From behind Sara, Randall's voice boomed into the room. "Get on in here, Mary. Just because you were born in a barn don't mean you have to keep Mrs. Winthrop's door wide open."

Mary looked past Sara's shoulder, flipped him the bird with a smile, then hobbled up and into the living room. Under her breath, she said to Sara, "You'd think he was fifteen years old some days."

"Do men ever really grow up?"

"Tell me about it."

"Thanks so much for coming over," Sara said. "I hate to spring this on you guys like this."

Mary hobbled along behind Sara, following her into the kitchen where Randall sat at the table with the security information displayed in front of him. She said, "I wouldn't say you sprung it on us. I'm guessing you found out that Randall already knew?"

"Yes."

"Yeah, well, your folks gave me a heads up as well about a week after him."

"Those sneaky little…"

Mary grabbed Randall's baseball cap and slapped him on top of the head with it. "Bro-in-law, how are you?"

"Fine until you got here," he replied, but the remark was accompanied by a heavy smirk.

Sara offered to get them drinks or something to eat—she'd learned the hospitable southern gesture; offer regardless, even if your guests recently walked out of a ten-course Thanksgiving meal. Mary declined, Randall asked for a glass of water, and then they sat around the table. Sara left the blueprints in front of him and pulled up a chair for Mary.

"So, can I officially hire you to help us out for a couple of weeks? At least until they catch the people who might be coming after me? Randall says you're definitely the best—"

"He lies a lot."

"Don't bring that up again."

"Bring up what?" Sara asked.

"Remember those long stories? That one's longer. And she'll never let me live it down."

Mary reached over with her cane and bonked Randall on the head. "I like watching him squirm, that's all."

Sara let it go. She was curious about what'd happened between them, but currently, her own past was out there hunting her down with bared fangs and razor-sharp claws. She said, "That's funny. But look, before we even get started, let me say that… I know, God, I know how unreasonable this is and believe me, I'd never ask this of…well, *strangers*…not in a million years, but I have a feeling—my fear is—this is going to turn into something that either *shouldn't* involve the local police, or it'll be too big for them to handle. I'm not saying they're not good at their jobs, but I doubt that around here, they've probably never encountered anyone like Shelley Sergeant or Patty Kellog. If you're willing, Mary, I can make it worth your while. You, too, Randall. I've got money. Too much of it, so you can name your price. Five times your normal rate. Ten times. Whatever. Your call."

She watched as Mary and Randall exchanged glances. The look that passed between them suggested something that Sara couldn't quite place.

Mary said, "Your folks moved down here, what, about twenty years ago?"

"Little less. They came here after I graduated high school and left for college. Why?"

"They're two of the sweetest people I've ever met, Sara."

"Same here," Randall added.

"They're practically family. And I always offer the family discount."

"How much?"

"We'll call it even at a bottle of Jim Beam."

"What? I can't let you do that."

"No ifs, ands, or buts, and don't argue with me, because we've got work to do."

Sara huffed, but knew she wasn't going to change their minds. "Sure, okay. If you say so."

Mary leaned up on the table and pulled the blueprints over in front of her. Seconds later, she whistled, long and high. "Would you look at that? Randall, you didn't say I'd be staking out Fort Knox."

"Better for you to make that assessment yourself. Keeps you on your toes."

Curious, Sara said, "So the system's good then?"

"*More* than good."

"Great, because really, all I did was track down the best security company I could find and throw a crap ton of money at them. Top of the line, spare no expense and whatever. I bought the place and we stayed with my parents while they were installing it, so I never completely saw everything as it was installed. All I wanted to know was what buttons to push and when. By the time they were finished, the owner of the company called me personally to say I was better protected than Tom Cruise."

"No kidding. Tom Cruise?"

"Apparently they have a lot of famous clients, but yeah, I guess that gives you a frame of reference, huh?"

"I wouldn't even need to hear that to know this is a fortress. Did you see this, Randall?" Mary pointed to a series of lines surrounding the perimeter of the house.

"I sure did."

"What're you looking at?" Sara asked.

"Oh, just the three-inch steel rods implanted along this line here with your fence and the laser beams along the top of it. I've seen this in movies, but never real life."

"Those are good, too, right?"

"You've got more than a panic room, sweetie, you've got a panic *house*."

TEN

Patty parked the car in the gravel driveway, which was pockmarked by craters of mud puddles and deep ruts from the runoff. Unlike back near the main road, where everything was slightly damp, it had rained here recently, and water dripped from the maple leaves overhead.

Her senses were still tingling from Shelley's kiss, but she tried not to let it show. Had she wanted it to happen? Yes and no. She had no time to think about it now. Analyzing it would have to come later. Shelley had pulled away, traced her thumb across Patty's bottom lip, and said nothing more. They'd ridden in silence after that.

Shelley craned her neck to see out the front window, looking up at the top level of the three-story farmhouse. "This place looks like there should be crazy people on the front porch, picking banjos."

"Don't let it fool you. The guys in there? I would *not* want to piss them off."

"Why?"

"You'll see, but let me tell you this... I've been all around the world. I've worked jobs for some scary human beings. I've *killed* some scary human beings. I've traded illegal arms and done recon work for people that would put a knife in your throat if you didn't laugh at their jokes fast enough, but honest to God, these backwoods, southwest Virginia rednecks scare me just as bad as the Mexican cartels."

"Really?"

"Take a look around, Shelley. Out here, they'd never find your body." Patty pointed around the yard's perimeter. Past the rusted swing set, past the old Chevy pickup that sat on cinderblocks, missing its tires, and past the gray-wood shed that would fall over in a strong gust of wind. "That's miles and miles of thick forest out there and these guys know all the best places to bury bodies. Trust me."

"Then why're we here?"

"We're picking up supplies." Patty opened her door and climbed out of the rental car. Her back and legs ached from the long flight and the ensuing drive, but she dared not relax long enough to stretch. "Don't say a word. You let me talk. Don't do anything but stand there and look…"

Shelley pointed at her disfigured face. "Pretty?"

"I was going to say confident, but whatever floats your boat."

Patty headed across the wet yard. The grass hadn't

been mowed in a while and the dampness soaked into her shoes. She shivered against the moist chill. Her black t-shirt and gray cargo pants didn't provide much protection against the cool mountain climate.

Rain dripped from the leaves overhead. She pushed the tire swing to her side, held it for Shelley, and continued. A bright red tricycle lay overturned next to a child's sandbox peppered with cat turds and twigs. They stepped around it and kept going. Shelley cursed when she slipped on a baseball bat hidden in the grass.

They went up the creaking stairs, then across the sagging porch to the front door. Three rocking chairs sat empty to their left, and on their right, a porch swing hung from a single chain. The other had snapped and dangled, swaying in the breeze.

"Why's it so quiet?" Shelley asked, looking through the small windows beside the door.

"I don't know. I've only been here a couple of times, but normally they greet me with a shotgun in one hand and a jar of moonshine in the other."

"Are they gone? Did they know you were coming?"

"They know. I paid them too much not to know."

Patty lifted her hand to knock. After two quick raps on the door, she heard a familiar sound behind them and down in the yard. A racking shotgun, instantly recognizable.

"Hands on your heads, ladies." The voice was rough and deep with a thick Appalachian drawl.

Patty lifted her arms and locked her fingers behind her head. She risked a peek to the right to make sure Shelley was doing the same. Thankfully, her arms were up as ordered.

Patty said, "Bobby? Is that you?"

"Yes, ma'am. You carrying, Kellog?"

"No. Same rules apply, as always. Left everything in the car. You can check if you want."

"Who's your friend?"

Patty heard the voice getting closer as he stealthily approached them from the rear. "My new partner."

Partner? Really? Yeah, well, easier to explain than…whatever Shelley is.

"Since when do you roll with anybody that ain't your lap dog, huh?"

"She's good. Trust me."

"I can trust her? Well thanks so much for letting me know. Now I'm all hunky-dory comfortable with you bringing a goddamn stranger to my house." The voice was ascending the porch now. Patty considered turning around.

Too risky, she thought. *Wait for the okay.*

116

"I'm vouching, Bobby. Say hello to Shelley Sergeant. They call her Sarge."

"They do, huh? Sounds like an awful big name for such a little girl. Turn around, both of you. Hands right where they are."

Patty turned clockwise, and Shelley turned counter-clockwise, in slow, cautious circles until they faced Bobby.

His head rocked back and his eyebrows arched. "Whoa," he said. "The hell happened to you, girl?"

Shelley shrugged. "Bar fight."

"Jesus. Did you win?"

"You should see the other guy."

Bobby smirked and lowered his shotgun. Lowered only—the barrel remained pointing at their midsections. "She telling the truth, Sarge? I can trust you?"

Shelley added a thick drawl to her words, saying, "You sure can, sweetheart."

Bobby leaned back and examined her with a yellow-toothed grin. "Are you mockin' me, young lady?"

"I thought I was flirting."

"Good enough." To Patty, he said, "I like her, Kellog. Keep her around a while."

"I plan to." Patty hadn't seen Bobby in five years,

since the job in Atlanta with that stubborn CEO that had to be forcefully removed, and the surly redneck hadn't changed at all. His hair was slicked back into a thick shell covering his scalp. The thin beard looked as scraggly as it always had, while the only noticeable difference was the fact that his neck tattoo of a scorpion seemed slightly more faded. He wore a red Harley-Davidson t-shirt, a leather vest, and blue jeans with holes at the knees, along with cowboy boots made out of some exotic hide. She was fairly sure he'd been wearing the same thing the last time they'd met.

She said, "You look good, Bobby."

"I liked your hair longer."

Patty flicked her chin over her shoulder, toward the entrance. "Is he here?"

"Pops?" Bobby clicked his tongue and shook his head. "You don't call, you don't write…"

"What happened?"

"Heart attack. Sumbitch dropped in the shower while we were all down at the Wal-Marts. I'm running the show 'round here now."

"I'm sorry for your loss."

"Me, too," Shelley added.

Arnold Davis, Bobby's father, also known as Papa Bear, was likely the meanest, most ruthless man Patty had ever met. She'd heard stories of worse individuals, but not many. Once, when she'd stopped by for a fresh supply of weaponry, she'd found the whole family in the middle of a revenge party. Out back, Papa Bear had tied an enemy to a clothesline pole and unleashed his pack of starving hounds on the unfortunate bastard. Patty hadn't been able to watch the frenzy. She'd turned her head away while Papa Bear ate a medium-rare steak and laughed with his mouth full.

When the dogs had had their fill, Papa Bear tossed the remnants into a wood chipper, along with the rest of his uneaten steak. That spectacle had been one of the worst things she'd seen and made her reconsider ever coming back. But, the Davis family had connections and sold their wares cheaply—plus, they'd go to their graves with their client list. That southern honor and dependability was something Patty could count on, knowing that the FBI or ATF, whomever, would have to bring in the National Guard to attempt a raid on the compound.

However, she didn't know if it was a good thing, or a bad thing, that Papa Bear was gone and Bobby was now in charge. She'd seen signs over the years that Bobby had the potential to be worse than his father.

"Really, Bobby," she lied, "he was a good man."

Bobby lifted a shoulder, let it drop. "Eh, well, shit happens, huh? Y'all come on in." He pushed past them and opened the front door. "Mind your dirty feet, and put your damn hands down. You look ridiculous."

Inside the old farmhouse, the smell was unbearable. Patty knew immediately that it was the stench of death. Shelley lifted her arm to cover her nose, and Patty pulled it down, shaking her head. Whatever the source, she didn't want to risk offending Bobby. She glanced around the room, looking for maybe a dead cat or dog and saw only deteriorating furniture and fast food bags littering the floor. Half-eaten cheeseburgers accompanied french fries and smeared ketchup on paper plates. The to-go soda cups littered on the coffee table had soaked through and the most recent ones had puddles of melted ice corralling the discolored bottoms.

Papa Bear, despite his hardened heart and corroded psyche, had loved tending to the variety of plants that once sat vibrant and lively around the living room. Patty remembered that each one had a name, and he'd coo at them like children while he spritzed water from a bottle. She'd been absolutely flabbergasted watching the display, then reassured of the man she knew when he held a knife against her cheek and demanded more money for the items she'd ordered.

That was what, nine years ago?

Those same plants were dry, brown, and dead, but they weren't the source of the smell.

Beside her, she could hear Shelley trying desperately not to dry heave.

As if he'd sensed their discomfort, Bobby rested the shotgun on his shoulder, turned, and said, "Don't mind the smell. Mama Bear ain't had time to bury the old man yet." And as they entered the kitchen, he added, "But you'll get around to it, won't you, Mama?"

Shelley gagged.

Patty swallowed and tried desperately to keep her composure.

Sitting at the table, or propped up, rather, was the body of Papa Bear Davis. Patty didn't have much experience with corpses, beyond being in the same room when her target became one, but she guessed he'd been there a while. It was impossible to guess how long.

To his right sat Myrtle Davis, also known as Mama Bear, and the only woman Patty had ever met that was more intense, determined, and evil than herself. But, gone was the woman that Patty respected and honored and in her place sat a nearly catatonic vessel of what had been. Myrtle's skin was sallow and sagging. The light brunette color of her hair had changed to a cloudy white. Her hand shook as she absently shoveled a forkful of scrambled eggs into her mouth.

She didn't look up, and she didn't acknowledge them when Bobby said again, "I *said*, you'll get around to it, won't you, Mama?"

When he slapped her on the back of the head, Patty felt a rush of anger warm her belly, and she had to resist fighting back for Myrtle's sake. Shelley took a quick step forward and Patty put a cautioning arm in front of her.

Shelley pursed her lips, scrunched her forehead, and mouthed, "Let me."

Patty shook her head.

Bobby leaned down and shouted, "Why don't you get up and get us something to drink, huh? Where's your manners, old woman?"

Myrtle put her fork down, stood up, and went to the refrigerator. She opened the door and stood, waiting.

"Y'all want something?" Bobby asked. "Beer? We got all kinds of pop, too."

"No, thanks," Patty said. "Maybe we could—how about you just give us what I came for and we'll get out of your hair, huh? Sound good?"

"What's your hurry, Kellog? Pops ain't gonna bother you none, not like that time he almost cut your cheek off. Remember that? Mean old codger, wasn't he? Take a load off and sit a spell."

"We're up against a timeline, Bobby. Sorry."

"Suit yourself. Beer, Mama." When Myrtle handed him the bottle, he popped the top and motioned for them to follow him down the shadowy hallway on the far side of the kitchen. "It's all down here. Y'all come take a gander."

Patty took a deep breath. It'd been so long since she'd been on this side of fear.

Shelley grabbed her hand and squeezed as they followed Bobby into the darkness.

ELEVEN

Sara greeted Teddy coming in from their hike as he sat down at the kitchen table with her, Randall, and Mary Walker. A moment later, Irina joined them and asked what all the schematics and blueprints were for.

Sara answered, "Randall and Mary have agreed to help out until the police manage to catch Shelley, so we're looking over the security measures that I already have in place here and trying to decide whether or not we need anything extra."

Teddy leaned up onto the table with his chin resting between his thumb and forefinger, looking over the drawings. "Something was bothering me while we were out for a walk, but I'd like to hear what you guys have been talking about first before I bring it up."

Mary said, "Well, from what we can see, she's almost completely covered. It's insane the amount of protection she has set up here, but we've noted a couple of vulnerable spots that Randall and I aren't quite comfortable with."

"Such as?"

"Mainly from overhead. The system they installed covers the perimeter so well that I doubt anyone would be able to get in here undetected. On foot, I mean. With cameras here, here, and here," she said, continuing around the diagram of Sara's property, "they'd have to be invisible to sneak through. There are regular cameras that are also accompanied by thermal cameras and over here at the gate entrance—if they manage to get *through* the gate—there's a pressure sensitive indicator built into the driveway…"

"What if they don't knock before they come in?"

"The fencing around the perimeter of the property has lasers from post to post, and then in a grid running along the top bar. Nothing is getting through or over that fence without something being triggered."

"Yeah, I know that. Sara showed me earlier, but what I meant was—you said there were vulnerabilities from above, right? Exactly what are you expecting? I'm assuming a coordinated air strike is out of the question." Teddy grinned.

Mary studied him, then glanced over to Sara. "You were right."

Teddy's smile faded. "About what?"

When everyone around the table finished chuckling, Irina bent over, put a hand on one cheek, and then kissed him on the other. "That *you*, dear husband, are a piece of work."

"Figures. Look, I'm just trying to help out."

Sara gave him a reassuring pat on the back. "We know, buddy, but I think Mary and Randall have this under control. She was a police officer for a long time and runs her own private investigation firm. They've been through quite a bit together and I trust them."

"I'm only looking out for you."

"And I understand that. But hey, what were you thinking about on your hike?"

Teddy sighed and shook his head. "Here's the thing. Going out on a limb, say that Patty Kellog is actually helping Shelley and they're on their way here. More than likely, Patty's got her own team with her, they've got all kinds of gadgets or whatever… You may be better protected than Tom Cruise, but I don't think Tommy Boy has a paramilitary terrorist group with access to high-tech toys trying to break into his compound, you know? Everything you have set up here, there are ways around it."

Randall reached over the table, with a long, massive arm that didn't need much stretching to cover the distance, and socked Teddy on the shoulder. "We know that, T-bird, so what we need to figure out is how they'd get around it. You've been around video games your whole life, designing them, helping with the stories—let's look at it this way. If you were creating a scene in *Juggernaut* where your horde of goons had to assault a fortress like this, how would you get into it?"

Teddy pulled the property schematics closer for a better look. He chewed on his bottom lip and said, "I honestly don't know. If we knew what was out there on the market right now... They could have one of those electro-magnetic pulse things to knock out your electronics, they could have something to disable the laser grid, who knows. Regardless of what they have, nothing is getting past the motion detectors short of disabling the system, so yeah, they'll have to hit hard and fast instead of sneaking onto the property. I guess like Miss Walker was saying, the vulnerabilities are from overhead. Or, below, supposing they wanted to tunnel underneath the fence."

Sara shook her head. "There's a wall of concrete that extends five feet underneath the surface."

"Christ on a corndog," Randall said. "How much did that set you back? You know, never mind, that was rude of me to ask."

"Doesn't matter," Teddy answered for her. "She can afford it. Anyway, yeah, so if tunneling is out, then all we have left is overhead."

"And how would you go about that?"

"You mean aside from the aforementioned air strike?" He flinched when Irina lifted her hand and playfully smacked his cheek. "Chill, okay? I'm kidding. Helicopter?"

"Too much noise, but *maybe*," Randall said. "Sara, you've heard them come through here before, haven't you?"

"At least two or three times a week."

Randall pointed behind him, toward the southwest, and brought his hand up, over, and pointed toward the northeast as he said, "We're right in the flight path from that big ass hospital down in Johnson City, coming and going. It wouldn't seem too out of the ordinary to have a chopper take that route and pause long enough for a commando team to repel down."

"Could be," Mary said. "Teddy's right, though, they'd likely hit hard and fast because they'll either have done their homework, or they'll assume motion sensors are a part of the package. If they came flying over disguised as a medical chopper, they could drop onto the roof before we even figured out what was going on."

Randall nodded. "True, true."

Irina raised her hand.

Teddy said, "Honey, you don't have to do that. Just ask."

"All of these plans, plans, plans—are you positive

she's coming to this place? Here is what I see—forgive me for butting in, but Teddy has told me what he knows about the history with this Shelley person—"

"And Patty Kellog, too."

"Yes, her, but what I see is a bunch of planning for something that may never happen. What if this Shelley person and this Patty person, what if they have nothing to do with each other and you're worrying yourselves to death over nothing? My grandfather had a saying back in Russia: 'Don't drink the vodka before the potatoes are grown.' Does that make sense here?"

"It does, ma'am," Randall said, "but when it comes to shit like this, it ain't possible to be *too* prepared."

Sara listened to them chat back and forth, smiling at the differences between Irina's Russian accent and Randall's mountain twang. It felt good to have so many people looking out for her. It was reassuring. Her own little United Nations.

And maybe Irina was right. Maybe she'd misheard back in Jim Rutherford's house and maybe Shelley being rescued from prison didn't have anything to do with her or Patty Kellog.

Was she getting worked up over nothing?

She got her answer when Barker called a minute later.

***

Sara checked the caller ID while the others were chatting. "Whoa," she said, holding out her phone. "It's Barker."

Teddy said, "Nice. Maybe he's got some good news."

"I'll put it on speaker. Give me a sec." She answered. "Barker, thank God. Tell me something good."

"Hey, Sara. You okay out there?"

"No, I'm freaking out. Hold on, okay? I'm going to put you on speaker so everyone else can hear you." She pushed a button and sat the phone down in the middle of the table. "Still there?"

"Yeah."

"Good. Let me introduce everyone—"

"You got an army there?"

"Teddy and Irina, plus I have my neighbor Randall who's a former Marine sniper, and his sister-in-law Mary Walker. She used to be a police officer and now she has her own P.I. business."

"Damn. You've already assembled your own team, huh? Well, except for Teddy, right? You got him carrying water for everybody else?"

Teddy snorted. It was something between an

annoyed scoff and a laugh. "I'm right here, Barker. I can hear you."

"You were meant to, bud."

Sara said, "We saw you at the press conference. Kinda freaked me out when we heard that Shelley was the one who escaped. We're here planning for the worst unless you have something good to report." Her tone was optimistic. On the inside, she was begging for anything positive.

"I'm…" Barker paused.

His tone, the elongated silence, waiting, waiting, Sara realized that he was about to crush her hopes.

"It's not looking good, Sara. The moment I found out it was Shelley that escaped, I got in touch with Agent Morrow and jumped right on this because I knew you'd want me to, and I'm afraid that what we're dealing with is bigger than what the press conference let on. At least when it comes to *you*."

"Meaning what?"

"It's—"

Sara's lungs cinched tighter. She closed her eyes and felt her skin prickle. "It's Patty Kellog, isn't it?"

"I'm afraid so."

Dizzy, Sara sat forward in her seat, rubbing her temples.

For the love of God, this can't be happening again.

Teddy asked, "How do you know that for sure?"

"This doesn't leave your house, okay? Everyone there understand that?"

A chorus of affirmative responses went around the table.

"I could potentially lose my job for even saying anything, but you need to know. Now, granted, I didn't expect an audience but I can't dangle the carrot and let it go, especially with what sounds like a good crew you got there." He cleared his throat. "Okay, here's the deal, folks. Since Patty Kellog escaped after Jim's house went boom, the FBI formed a small task force, maybe a two or three man team, but nothing big, see?

"Patty was low on the totem pole as far as international priorities go, but the suits wanted her gone, mostly because of the bullet she'd put into Timms. Anyway, these cats rounded up a couple of dudes that were former military and sent them undercover. I mean, Jesus, from what they tell me, these guys were so far under that they almost started believing the propaganda themselves. It was like a global chess match for about eight months, but the FBI managed to work these guys into Patty's good graces. Their orders were to gather intel on her movements and whatnot so they could put together a case against her. The feds were going for a prosecution, but if it'd been me, I would've had one of those gents slip a knife in between her ribs."

Randall bent over, closer to the phone. "Detective Barker?"

"Yes, sir?"

"Randall Blevins here. So what I'm hearing is, the FBI had someone in close proximity to Patty Kellog, like within breathing distance, and this bullshit at the prison *still* went down? That's what I'm hearing?"

"You'll never hear them admit to it, but they really screwed the pooch on this one. From what they could gather, these two guys—their names were Crenley and Tanner—they'd had intel on a different job. Patty had them thinking they were going after some big-time CEO up here in the northwest, sort of a corporate espionage thing. We don't know if she was onto them or if she changed her mind at the last minute. Whatever the case, evidently these guys had no clue that they were about to break into a prison to get Shelley Sergeant out. It's Morrow's assumption that they went through with it to keep from breaking cover."

"That's great," Sara said, her hope returning. "If that's the case, then they're right on top of her and we don't have anything to worry about, do we?"

"That's what I called to tell you. We have *everything*

to worry about now."

"What? Why?"

"A Mickey D's employee found Tanner and Crenley in the dumpster about an hour ago. Looks like one of them might've been wounded during the prison break and maybe Patty finished him off with a single shot. The other one had two in the forehead. Dead and gone. Surveillance cameras show two women dumping the bodies but they're masked and we couldn't identify them. But, from what I've seen before, their physical builds seem to be about right for your two supervillains. Cameras show them driving off and heading east. No make on the license plates and we think, stressing the *think* here, that they're responsible for the two scientists that the reporter mentioned during the news conference. I mean, hell, we're lucky the supervisor went looking for those two so he could warn them about the incoming weather, otherwise, they might not have found the bodies for weeks."

"So what're you saying, Barker? Am I really hearing you right? Patty and Shelley are definitely together?"

"It looks to be that way."

"And you have no clue where they are now? Other than the fact that they were heading east to God-knows-where?"

"The feds are checking into a couple of hotline tips where people think they might've seen the blue Explorer. Aside from that, they're chasing tails. It's a goddamn shitshow in the office over there. I had to sneak out to call you."

"Why?"

"Morrow knows about your history with both of these ladies and in case they *are* heading your way, rather than sending in protection like I begged him to do over and over, he's adamant about holding back. If they're coming to your house, he doesn't want a bunch of suits hanging around the farm to tip them off. He'll have eyes on you from a distance—maybe satellites or a drone, something—but nobody on the ground except for a couple of guys in a car.

"He *says* he'll make a move before they can get close enough, but his goal is to take her alive somewhere between here and there. The way he sees it, they'll screw up before they get out of the state and I'm inclined to agree with him."

"We figured that much, too," Randall said, "but that still don't explain why he's not protecting Sara *here*."

"Your guess is as good as mine. Patty's got her Boudica cover spread all around the world and he wants her to snitch on some big names. Guy's got a real hard-on for making a name for himself. You know the type. He tells me I'm on a need-to-know and promises you'll be safe, but you can put a promise on a scale and see how much it weighs. Stinks to high heaven to me, but he swears they'll never get close to you."

"And I'm supposed to be reassured by that?"

"I know, I know, I'm not a fan of it either."

Sara sat back, limp and defeated. She looked around the table.

Teddy shook his head. Irina chewed a fingernail. Mary and Randall exchanged glances.

Barker added, "As shitty as that is, we don't know one hundred percent for certain that they're even coming in your direction. Tanner and Crenley had reported back a couple of times and mentioned that Patty had a ton of work lined up for them down in South America. Could be—and this is a strong possibility—she broke Shelley out so that crazy-ass girl could go work for her. We don't know that, but it seems plausible. As of thirty minutes ago, we're looking into any possible leads until something solid turns up."

Randall said, "Let me ask you something, Detective."

"Sure thing."

"Sara told me the history between 'em all... Where do you put the odds that those two are coming here to finish the job? Honestly. No bullshit."

"Honestly? I wouldn't bet against it."

TWELVE

Patty walked slowly, allowing Shelley to keep her grip around her wrist.

They had followed Bobby down the dark hallway, reached a set of stairs, and descended into what felt like a cold Hell. Once they'd reached the bottom, orange lights illuminated the walls, casting a fiery glow, even though her skin prickled from the chill.

Bobby whistled as he strolled, shotgun resting lazily on his shoulder; just another day at the office for this hillbilly with too much power and not enough sense, while his father rotted upstairs and his mother slipped further into madness.

Inside her left pocket, she carried a small knife, disguised to look like a tube of lip balm. She slid her hand in and felt the cylindrical object. It wasn't much, but with enough force and enough repetition, she could easily get enough jabs into Bobby's neck to send him where his father had already gone.

The only downside to that plan was the fact that she'd been down here before, with Papa Bear, and knew that the door at the far end was equipped with an electronic security system. She'd need the code to get the door open, and Bobby was insane enough to allow her the pleasure of torturing him without ever giving it up. The way Myrtle had checked out of reality, she'd never get a response from her either.

When they reached the end and turned the corner, she learned that it wouldn't have mattered anyway.

Things had changed since she'd been down here last. An entire metal wall with a sliding door system had replaced the original metal door, which had been controlled by a six-digit entry code.

Patty had to stop herself from whistling. It was fancy and expensive for the backwoods in southwest Virginia. How much had it set them back? A million? More? To look at this family, it would never be apparent that they were worth millions themselves. They'd served as a mid-point, illegal arms dealer up and down the east coast for decades.

From what she'd been told, back in the seventies, Papa Bear had somehow wormed his way into the trade. He staged a rights grab on what entered and exited his territory, and a few dead bodies later, the Cuban drug lords in Florida and the mafia bosses in New York appeased him after their failed attempts to eliminate the pesky bastard.

The couriers that had tried to slip by undetected learned the hard way that crossing him was not a viable option. He made Vlad the Impaler look like a Sunday school teacher.

Where Papa Bear operated within some level of controlled chaos, Bobby had always been the one to serve *as* the chaos. And it was infinitely more disturbing now that he was in charge of what remained.

Patty shivered.

Bobby stepped to the side, pushed three green buttons, and waited on a panel to slide open in the wall. "Ain't that some shit?" he asked. "Watch this." He put his face up to the exposed hole and said, "Entry."

Patty listened to the sound of whirring gears. A blue stream of light emanated from the opening, traveled up Bobby's left eye, and then down.

Something inside the wall beeped twice, and Bobby repeated, "Entry."

A thinner, flat panel slid forward. He placed his hand on the black surface. Two more beeps, followed by the sounds of releasing latches, then hissing pistons, as the door slid open from the middle. It retracted into the wall's sides.

Whatever lay beyond was covered in a darkness so deep that Patty could see nothing beyond the spot where the orange hallway lights could reach.

Shelley squeezed Patty's hand once and let go, moving backward and then sidestepping behind her.

Bobby snickered. "Damn, girl, don't be scared. It's just a warehouse." Then to Patty, he added, "What do you think about that system, Kellog? That's some James Bond stuff, huh? Voice recognition, eyeball scanner, and not only does that panel check the fingerprints, it matches the oils in your skin to what it has on file. Ain't got no idea how all them contraptions works, but the goddamn President of the United States couldn't get in here."

She'd seen systems that were more impressive, especially in Eastern Europe, but she wasn't going to tell Bobby that. "It's amazing. What happened to the old door, the one with the code panel?"

"About a year ago, Daddy had a close call with the ATF and got a little paranoid. *Loco* in the *cabeza*. So, he had this system right here put in, figuring that if he ever took a ride to the big house, none of those pricks would be able to get in here to confiscate his stash." He flicked his chin toward the entryway, cradling the shotgun at chest level. "After you."

Patty could feel the hesitation in Shelley without looking at her. She had a bit of it herself, but she knew that what Bobby enjoyed more than killing people were people that gave him a lot of money. "Is it all in there?"

"Go on and see for yourself."

She took a deep breath and stepped forward. Once she'd passed the threshold, motion sensors detected her presence and bright, fluorescent bulbs flickered on overhead. She squinted against the light as it revealed row upon row of shelving, filled with boxes, pelican cases, and all forms of ammunition containers along the right hand side. On the left, weapons hung on pegs, all the way down to the end of the tunnel some fifty feet away. M-16s, sniper rifles, AK-47s, grenades attached to belts—it was a complete arsenal, enough to put some sort of deadly device in every hand of a small militia.

This time, Patty *did* whistle. The storage room had evolved since she'd been there last and she had to admit, the collection was impressive. Though it wasn't necessarily a collection, considering the fact that every item in there was on its way to somewhere else. It was backstock awaiting delivery.

Bobby pointed to a gold-plated 9mm Glock hanging close to Patty's shoulder. "You see that gorgeous sumbitch right there? Guess where that's going."

"Disney World."

"Hah, funny, but nope. That pretty little piece of jewelry is on its way down to Juarez. Carlos motherlovin' Jimenez. Can you believe it?"

Patty couldn't hide her surprise. "El Toro?"

"I call him El Caca de Toro, but not to his face." He glanced around at Shelley and grinned at her. "That means 'the bull shit' if you don't know *espanol*."

Shelley spoke for the first time since they'd entered the house. "I know what it means, *puto*."

The last word rattled Bobby. He stepped closer. "What'd you say to me?"

"Easy," Patty said, holding up a hand. "She called you a friend, that's all."

"You sure about that? Because I had a pretty little Mexican *mamacita* call me that same thing one time, only she didn't have a smile on her face. And you want to know what happened to her? I carved a smile for her. She's just like the Joker now, always grinning, ear to ear."

Patty tried to change the subject. "What're you doing with El Toro's Glock, Bobby? I thought the Juarez guys ran stuff through Albuquerque."

"He's setting up some operations with the Tarantino family in Yankee Town. Glock's a gift from one peckerwood to another. It's hanging out here for a few days like a show pony down at the county fair."

144

"So you're big time now, huh? Rubbing elbows with some of the worst badasses in two countries?" She was trying to butter him up. Bobby had always been hasty with the temper, but he was prone to having his ego stroked.

"You know how Daddy was. He got his business to where he wanted it and got lazy. There ain't no challenge when everybody's sucking at your teat already. I told him—I told him for years that we could do more, but no sir, he wasn't having it. I was 'bout damn sick of it, to tell you the truth, and if the heart attack hadn't gotten him, I wasn't too far from sending him down the road a ways myself."

Patty shrugged. "Don't make no never mind now, does it?" She'd heard the country slang once before, in some movie, and had always wanted to try it out. It felt strange rolling off her tongue, like the words had gotten mixed up somewhere in her throat.

Bobby grinned. "No, ma'am, it don't."

He glanced away, down toward the end of the room, and Patty thought she saw him lick his lips. Maybe they were dry. Maybe she could offer him the business end of the lip balm in her pocket. Or maybe he had something else in mind. Her intuition tingled with the latter—she could feel his intent, whatever it was.

***

Patty stood in front of a waist-high metal table, about the size of a hospital gurney, looking over the equipment she'd ordered months ago. Finally, it had all arrived two weeks prior—some of it bought easily on the black market, some of it custom-made—and she'd gotten the call from Bobby to come pick it up. The timing was perfect, coinciding with Shelley's escape, and Patty was thankful for it. She'd been contemplating what they could've done in the meantime.

Bobby said, "Took me a while, but it's all here. Let's tick things off the checklist to make sure it's everything you ordered."

"I trust you."

"You damn well better, but this is how I run things, though, and you'd be wise to play along."

"Gotcha."

The first item he grabbed was a pair of military-grade night vision goggles, the hands-free kind that could easily tighten around various head sizes. "Five pairs of night vision specs. Standard issue, no big deal getting those."

"We only need two sets."

"You fire some people?"

"You could say that."

"I was wondering where the rest of your crew was. The order stands, Kellog. You wanted five, you're paying for five."

Patty nodded. She'd expected that. Still, it never hurt to try. Over the years, she'd found that she could bargain with most folks if she was respectful. In a lot of countries, bargaining was customary and the selling party would get offended if you didn't try to haggle. Not here, though. Not in Papa Bear's, and now Bobby's, basement.

"Next, we got one laser doohickey. It's a…what is it? Hell if I remember what the damn thing is called. It breaks the beam without setting off an alarm, right?"

"Right."

"There you go. Next," he said, moving down the table, "you have five sets of various handguns, rifles, pistols, whatever—automatic, semi-automatic. This one right here would put a hole the size of a bowling ball through an elephant. I reckon you only need two sets, but you'll be taking all five with you, won't you?"

Patty nodded. From the corner of her eye, she could see Shelley crossing her arms and shaking her head, behind Bobby and out of his sight.

Not a word, Shelley. Just business.

Bobby moved to the last set of items on the table.

Five black bodysuits, folded neatly, as if they were on display at an Old Navy. She wondered if they came that way, or if Bobby had taken the time to fold them himself. "And these sumbitches... You have any idea how hard it was to get *one* of these damn things, much less five of them in five different sizes?"

Stepping up to the table, Shelley bent over and examined them. "What're those?"

Patty picked up the top one from the pile and shook it out. It looked like a surfer's wetsuit, except that it had fingers and toes. Once on, the only open spots were thin slits across the eyes. "Ambient temperature suits. With these things, we're practically invisible to a thermal camera."

Shelley said, "I didn't even know those existed."

"You'd be surprised what's out there."

"And why do we need all of this stuff? You said so yourself, the bitch lives in a damn farmhouse in the middle of nowhere. It's not like we're breaking into the CIA building." When Patty didn't immediately agree, Shelley added, "Right?"

Patty held up one of the suits and examined it in the light. She said, "No, but it's damn close."

THIRTEEN

Detective Emerson Barker walked into the task force office, feeling comfortable about Sara's situation all the way over in Virginia. With three thousand miles between her and the evil women—he hoped—it seemed like she was in good hands with an ex-cop and a former Marine Corps sniper standing by. And as much as it pained him to admit it, Teddy wasn't a slouch when it came to firing a weapon either. He'd seen the effects of it back in Jim Rutherford's house; the way Teddy hit his targets with such accuracy, he effectively saved a number of lives that day, including Barker's.

He'd never admit that Teddy had done such a thing, because the dude's ego already filled up every room he walked into, but at least Barker now considered him a friend. That was a far cry from having the over-privileged, junior Rutherford labeled as a kidnapping and murder suspect before he and DJ had discovered Shelley Sergeant was the culprit way back when.

Barker stood at the entryway, watching the spry and spotless agents buzz around him, going over files, surveying maps, and generally looking clueless. He was relieved that he'd been granted the privilege of helping out, by both sets of superiors, but at the same time, he knew he was a protruding nail, just waiting for a hammer to come along. Proceed wisely, cooperate, and with any luck learn enough to keep Sara and her kids safe in the process.

He offered a mock salute as Agent Grady Morrow approached him and handed over a sheet of paper.

"What's this?" Barker asked.

"Contact list for private flight companies within a six-hour radius. Get on the horn with each one of these and see if they had anyone going east, most likely in the northeast Tennessee and southwest Virginia areas."

"Those private ones don't have to file a flight plan, do they?"

"No, but they'll have a record of who was going where."

"And you think they risked the visibility of an *airport?* Even if they don't have to go through the main terminal for a private flight, that's a damn chancy move."

"You never know, Barker. You asked to help, this is what I've got."

Barker suspected he was being handed the busy

work while the actual FBI agents were out putting
boots on concrete, but for once, he didn't mind. He
hadn't healed completely yet, and this might be a good
time to take a breath. His wounds ached. His muscles
whined whenever he bent over or took a step, and if he
popped another Percocet, he'd likely be in for a long
snooze at his temporary desk. "All right then, Morrow,
I'll get on it."

Besides, even if he *were* annoyed by being handed
the shit jobs, he had a damn good idea where Kellog
and Sergeant were heading, and the possibility of
finding them through a scheduled private flight was
more productive than interviewing a McDonald's fry
cook who'd never seen a dead body before.

Last they'd heard, the blue Explorer had been
heading east, over the Cascades, and there weren't
many options on that side of the mountains. The small
regional airport in Redmond was the likeliest place,
along with an airfield about the size of a postage stamp
down in Bend. Either could easily accommodate a
hasty exit, but he decided to save those calls for last. In
case the blue Explorer was a decoy, or the witnesses
had reported the wrong vehicle, it made sense to rule
out the private flights in the immediate vicinity first.

He started with Portland and came away with
information regarding four different private flights, all

heading toward the east coast, but none of them were landing in the proper region, and none of them carried two women, one of whom was missing an eye.

The FBI's saving grace on this one would be the fact that Shelley Sergeant had taken such an ass-whipping when she first arrived at Coffee Creek two years ago. The resulting loss of an eye left her so easily identifiable that he was certain they'd get call after call tracing her path. It hadn't happened yet, but once the news propagated throughout the internet and made its way onto the nightly reports, they'd be on her in no time.

Until then, grunt work would have to suffice.

Next, he tried Eugene and came up with nothing, then the rest of the list, checking off the smaller fields as he went one by one. Almost all of them had private flights that left that morning, and some of them even had flights heading in the proper direction, but none carried the reprehensible cargo he was looking for.

With two options remaining, he felt like he was scratching the last two spots on a lottery ticket, hoping beyond hope that the gold bar in Box A matched the gold bar in Box B. Or whatever the hell happened on scratch tickets these days.

Again, the calls to the Redmond private airports offered nothing. Same story. Eastbound private flights, but none to Virginia or Tennessee. Barker cursed and slammed the phone down. He sat back in his chair, twisted the tips of his mustache, and popped a cinnamon-flavored toothpick in his mouth. He'd gone nearly a year now without smoking, but the longing had never fully disappeared, especially when he was annoyed and needed something to occupy his mind while he processed details.

The airfield in Bend was the least likely of the two central Oregon choices, primarily because of how tiny it was. He'd been through it before a couple of times, landing there on the way to hunting and fishing trips with some wealthy buddies who'd chartered flights for the fun of it, and taking a private plane out of there didn't make much sense. Too small, too few people, too easy to peg a one-eyed woman.

A small flicker in the back of his mind caused Barker to sit upright. He said "Hold on, now," and grabbed the list of companies offering flights. He checked their websites to confirm what he'd remembered. The first two didn't even have an office there at the airfield, and the latter three did, and they were stationed in separate buildings, with one of those being nothing more than a guy with a desk.

Now that he'd taken time to process the situation…a flight out of Bend seemed more possible than not. However, four of the companies didn't have planes in their hangers that were capable of making cross-country flights. Instead, they were puddle jumpers used for flights up to Portland or Seattle, maybe even quick weekend trips over to the Oregon coast.

Barker managed to be worried and relieved at the same time. One option left room for both.

He was worried that he'd wasted so many hours of fruitless calling—who knew where Kellog and Sergeant could be—but also relieved because maybe those two weren't on their way to Sara's farm. They could be, but if they'd chosen to drive, that left a lot of miles and a lot of time to make mistakes.

With one last number to go, he called Cascade Aviation and crossed his fingers, praying he'd find them, praying that he wouldn't. Either was acceptable.

"Thank you for calling Cascade Aviation, this is Maria, how many I help you?"

"Maria, this is Detective Emerson Barker with the Portland P.D. I'd like to ask you a couple of questions if you have a moment."

"Um…sure."

He could sense the hesitation in her voice. People got it no matter how he introduced himself—friendly or gruff—and they turned inward, worried they'd done something wrong that they didn't know about, or they were worried they'd been busted for doing something they knew they shouldn't. Hence the pause, hence the hesitation, contemplating which one of their friends or family members was the tattletale.

Barker said, "Your company offers private flights, correct?"

"Yes, sir."

"We're aware that your pilots aren't required to file FAA flight plans, but I'm sure that you have a record of incoming and outgoing schedules, payment transactions…is that also correct?" He knew the answer would be yes, but it was a simple way to get Maria into a comfort zone, giving her the opportunity to relax and answer the easy questions. He did it with every witness. Boost up their confidence, then weed out the information he needed. Worked every time.

Maria said, "Oh, absolutely, Detective. We run a tight ship around here. My husband and I haven't had a single issue with our recordkeeping in the last twenty years."

"So this is your company?"

"Don and I run it together—well, when he's around. If he's not skiing, he's out on the golf course, but, what're you gonna do, huh? Men are men."

"I hear that."

"What can I help you with? I know you didn't call to listen to me jabber about my husband."

"Well, ma'am, I'd have to say you're my last shot. I've called more numbers than I can count today and I swear I've got a blister on my dialing finger. Anyway, you mind telling me which flights of yours went out today?"

"Not *flights*. Flight. We sold off most of our fleet when the economy tanked—and when I say fleet, I mean three planes—so now we just run with the one. They landed at the Tri-Cities airport a couple of hours ago."

Barker's heartbeat jack-hammered in his chest. He exploded out of the desk chair and felt his skin get warm. His fingers shook a little around the pen in his hand. "You're talking about TRI, there near Bristol?"

"That's the one."

"Son of a...Maria, couple more questions."

"Everything okay?"

"Can you tell me who was on that plane?"

"I can assure you, Detective, we don't cater to—"

"Who were the passengers, Maria?"

Barker listened to some papers rustling in the background. He scanned the room of bustling feds and spotted Morrow talking to an equally well-dressed woman off in the corner. He caught Morrow's eye and frantically waved him over.

Maria said, "Let's see here. Flight was booked and paid for by a woman named Sharon Ellison, um...two passengers, both female. Paid by credit card. One-way flight to TRI near Bristol, Tennessee."

"They checked in, right? Any chance you saw them board that plane today?"

Maria sighed, "Believe it or not, Detective, my husband was here then. The one time he actually spent more than thirty minutes in the office while I had a dentist's appointment."

"Is he there now? Can I speak to him?"

"I'd imagine he's made it to the back nine at this point. Always got his phone off during the rounds, but I'd say you can probably reach him in a couple of hours."

"No, that'll be too late." Barker tapped his pen on the desk, thinking. "What about the pilots? Did they radio in? Give you any details about their passengers?"

"They checked in a couple of times, but didn't say anything about their passengers. Not that they usually do. Let me give you their cell numbers and you can give them a call. Would that work? I'm not sure how much else I can help."

"Perfect, thank you." He jotted down the numbers, shaking in anticipation.

He wondered if he should ask her for the credit card information related to Sharon Ellison, then decided it would be a waste of time and resources. If Maria didn't want to go that far in her generosity of supplying the information he needed, the subpoena would take too long and tell them little. Supposing it *was* Patty Kellog, the credit card would be stolen, fake, or untraceable. No use in having the hapless feds around him chasing more ghosts.

Barker thanked her, hung up, and immediately dialed the pilot's cell phone.

Morrow stopped in front of Barker's desk. "You got something?"

While he listened to the ringing, Barker said to Morrow, "Private flight out of Bend landed in northeast Tennessee about two hours ago. Company confirms that two women were on board."

The voice on the other end of the line said, "Jeff speaking."

Barker introduced himself and waded through the initial round of hesitation, joking around with the pilot and co-pilot, giving them a moment to shore up their composure. He said, "Three simple questions for you and Smiling Dave."

"We're ready, sir."

"First, did you have two female passengers on

your flight today?" Barker held his breath, waiting. This was it. While it was certainly possible that Kellog and Sergeant could make it back east a thousand different ways, he prayed to God that he could pinpoint their location with this one simple phone call.

"We did, definitely."

"Was one of them in her late thirties, brown hair, sort of muscular?"

"Yeah, she was. Kinda tall, too. And a little scary, actually."

Brother, you don't even know. "Excellent. Last question, and this is the most important one...was the woman with her missing her left eye?"

Barker hung up before the pilot could finish saying that she was attractive, even with a missing eye.

FOURTEEN

Patty loaded the supplies in the back of the rental car. She'd lost sight of Shelley, who'd been so disgusted by the smell of Papa Bear's decomposing body that she had to run around the back side of the house with her shoulders hunched and a hand over her mouth. Bobby had laughed, shaken his head, and offered to bring her a beer from the kitchen.

She took stock of everything to make sure they'd gotten it all, and her only regret was having to pay for all five sets of suits, night-vision goggles, guns and ammo. But, she could afford it, and perhaps the items might be used for future missions once she rebuilt her team.

She bent over to secure one of the Heckler & Koch 9mm semi-automatic handguns, her favorite of the bunch, and felt a presence behind her. An arm went around her stomach and another across her breasts. Something hard pressed against her backside and she immediately recognized what it was. Next came Bobby's heavy panting in her ear, followed by the pungent odor of alcohol on his breath.

"Watching you bend over like that got me all riled up, girl."

Patty slung an elbow at his ribs, felt the knife blade at her throat. "Get off me, Bobby."

"I don't think so. Not yet. I've been waiting for this for a long time. How long you been coming around here? Fifteen years? I've been holding myself back since the day you walked through that door because Daddy said so. 'No business with pleasure,' he said, which was bullshit to me, because it ain't work if it's fun. Ain't that right?"

Patty felt a hand on the button of her jeans, ripping it free, followed by a hard, rough tug at the zipper. The blade at her neck pressed a little deeper as he grabbed her jeans at the waist and yanked them down around her thighs.

She wasn't used to this. She didn't *experience* fear, she created it. What a strange sensation. It'd been so long. She was always so cool and collected, but now here she was, feeling that sense of impending dread in her stomach.

Patty considered screaming for Shelley, but Bobby was unpredictable and demented, and she wasn't so sure that being dead would make a difference in what he wanted from her.

He pulled her away from the car, grunting in her

ear as he tried to get his own jeans down. "Shut that damn trunk lid," he ordered, and Patty reluctantly obeyed. Bobby shoved her forward and she stumbled awkwardly into the car with her pants around her thighs. "Hands up in front of you."

The knife went back to her neck, and again, Patty did as she was told. She felt the blade pull across her skin ever so slightly. A warmness trickled down to her clavicle.

Bobby kicked at the insides of her feet, trying to get her legs apart.

Where are you, Shelley? Help me.

Patty whimpered and hated herself for it. She wasn't weak. This shouldn't be happening. She *made* people whimper. She'd watched grown men cry at her feet and beg for their lives. Was this retribution? Had karma finally caught up to her?

Had Shelley turned on her? Was that why she wasn't helping?

Patty strained to see the front porch through the car's rear window. A figure stood at the top of the stairs, but it wasn't Shelley. Myrtle stood like a porch column. Motionless. Blank faced. Unmoving. Only her nightgown rippled in the breeze. She watched them from her perch. Had Bobby brought her out or had she come to enjoy the scene on her own?

Bobby laughed and pressed himself against Patty's backside. "You ready, huh? You ready? Maybe when I'm done with you, I'll go find that one-eyed troll you brought with you. I ain't never been with no Cyclops before." He yelled up to Myrtle on the porch, "Ain't that what it's called, Mama? Them one-eyed things are called a Cyclops, right?"

Through the car window, Patty watched as Myrtle slowly lifted a shaky arm with a long, crooked finger, pointing at something. Not directly at them, but to the side, and Patty didn't have time to consider what the old woman was pointing at, because she felt the pressure between her legs; not entering, but there, and soon.

Vulnerable, that's what she felt. Vulnerable, exposed, and livid. She had worked hard to create a name, a worldwide reputation, and here she was, about to be violated by a backwoods redneck that she could've taken out with her pinky. But, she'd let her guard down and stopped paying attention for just the right amount of time. She should've known better, the way he was eyeing her and Shelley down in the basement. He *had* been licking his lips. She was sure of it now.

Grinding molar to molar, she inhaled deeply and waited. And then, from behind, she heard, "Wha—"

followed by a deep, throaty gurgling. The grip loosened at her waist and the knife fell away from her throat.

Next came Shelley's voice saying, "Die, hillbilly." *Thank God.*

Patty rolled over on the car's trunk, pulled her jeans up, and watched as Shelley shoved the bleeding man to the ground. He gagged on his own blood, clutching his throat, and tried to gasp for air. His eyes bulged and he tried to get to this feet. Shelley laughed, threw her leg back, and delivered a perfect kick to his ribs. Patty was certain she heard bones crunch. Bobby flopped over to his side, babbling, trying to say something.

"What's that?" Shelley asked. She kneeled down beside him, the blade in her hand wet and red. "I can't hear you." She giggled. "A little louder. Come on. You can do it." Taunting him with a devilish grin.

Patty watched Shelley toying with him. She was a cat with a wounded mouse, batting it around, playing with it before finishing it off. Patty bent over and grabbed the blade by the handle, taking it from Shelley's hand. "Give me that." Without hesitation, she buried it deep into Bobby's heart, yanked it free, and then marched through the yard. Up the steps to where Myrtle stood expressionless and nearly catatonic.

Patty drew the blade back, and in the second

before she struck, she swore she could see the sense of relief on the old woman's face. The blade slid between the ribcage easily, and Patty left it there when Bobby's mother fell. There would be no need for added insurance. Once would be enough, and chances were, the hag might die of the trauma before Bobby finished writhing on the ground. They were in a race to the end.

Patty spun around and found Shelley standing at the bottom of the steps with her arms crossed, wearing a smug, satisfied smile. Patty said, "What took you so long? I mean, Jesus H. Christ, he almost *raped* me. Where were you?"

Shelley dropped her arms and scowled. "That's what I get? I saved your life and you're scolding me?"

"Yeah, well, maybe you could've shown up a little bit sooner, huh?" Patty stormed down the stairs and used her shoulder to push Shelley out of the way. She made it two steps when she felt a hand on her wrist, and a pulling. With her nerves frayed, still charged on adrenaline, her instinct took over. She whipped around, grabbed Shelley's arm, bent low, pivoted, and threw her to the ground.

Shelley landed on her back, in the damp, muddy yard, and held up her hands in surrender as Patty dropped onto her, clutching the young woman's throat. There was real fear in Shelley's eyes.

Submission. "Don't," she said. "I was going to hug you and say I'm sorry."

Patty paused and loosened her grip. She sat back on her haunches.

Shelly continued, "If he'd seen me coming, he would've slit your throat. It took me a minute to get around the damn house and I thought for sure the old skeleton had given me away. So yeah, I'm sorry."

Patty leaned forward and stared into the single, beautiful eye. Her anger dissipated. "Next time, don't take so long." She kissed her, full on the lips, with tempered forgiveness. It felt good. Right and safe. When she pulled away, a slim string of saliva joined their lips. "Let's get out of here."

Shelley climbed up to her feet and tried to knock some of the damp grass off her sweater. Glancing down at Bobby's lifeless body, then up to Myrtle twitching on the porch, she asked, "What about these two?"

"Let them rot like his dad." Patty spat on Bobby then wiped her mouth with the back of a hand. "Maybe we should throw them in with the hounds around back."

"Too late," Shelley said. "They're all dead. That's how I got around back without them howling and giving me away."

"Doesn't matter. The crows will get them eventually."

"Should we try to salvage more of that stuff in the basement? He had enough to start an army."

Patty considered it, then remembered his security system, plus so much of the contents in there belonged to people she didn't want to mess with. It was fine if something happened to Bobby and his clients had no way of retrieving their cache, but if they found out it was gone, and she took it, there wouldn't be enough places to hide. "We're good," she said. "We'll only need what we have, and even that's more than enough."

They climbed in the car and when Patty backed up, they felt a satisfying thump as the tires rolled over Bobby. Killing him had multiple implications, but none that she wanted to concern herself with right now. They'd just eliminated one of the east coast's most well-known and trusted suppliers, which might ruffle some feathers, but at the same time, others might seek her out to offer thanks for knocking down the gates. It could go either way.

Regardless, it didn't matter. After their trip to Sara Winthrop's farm, she and Shelley would disappear, and there would never be a need to come this way again.

The rental car rattled and bounced down the

pothole-filled driveway, splashing muddy rainwater in low, arching fantails each time the tires dipped into a crater.

Shelley took Patty's hand and interlocked her fingers. "Hey."

"What?"

"I'm really sorry it took me so long."

"Don't worry about it."

"No, I'm serious. I don't know if I've, like, seriously thanked you for getting me out of prison, and for giving me a purpose, and for giving me another chance at Sara. You've done so much for me already."

"You're welcome."

"Why'd you do it?"

"Get you out?'

"Yeah."

Patty shrugged. "There's something evil underneath the human side of you. That's a good thing, and it'll take us far."

"Like how far?"

"Around the world. Warm places. Beaches. Sunshine. The Louvre and Prague and Thailand. Wherever we want to go. We're rare in this line of work—two women that are so...ruthless, I guess. We can bring top dollar simply because men are disgusting pigs, whether they're worth billions and sitting on a yacht off the coast of Fiji, or they're some primping coot in jolly old England. They get their rocks off knowing women are doing their work for them."

Shelley rolled her eyes. "That's not degrading at all."

"Looking at it from the outside, you could see it that way, but who's really getting the shaft when we're charging twice as much and knowing we can get away with it? We're playing with their egos, getting rich off their need to feel dominant without them even knowing we're pulling the strings. In a way, it's almost like watching porn, or strippers…who's screwing who?"

Patty stopped at the end of the driveway and waited on a rusted, rattling old pickup truck to lumber by. The driver took a look at them as he passed. Patty watched the aging farmer in his flannel jacket as he lifted a hand and waved.

Chances were, he was simply being friendly. People were like that around here. Stop to help somebody's grandmother change a flat tire along I-81, you became an honorary member of the family. Help your neighbor with his car in the snow, you'd earn a seat at Christmas dinner. On any other day, it wouldn't have been such a big deal, but due to nothing more than poor timing, he'd witnessed a rental car leaving

Bobby's property, and in a day or two when the bodies were discovered, he would easily remember something odd about that day.

She and Shelley exchanged knowing looks.

Shelley said, "Is it your turn or mine?"

Patty grinned and followed the old farmer. She said, "Yours, but don't be messy."

FIFTEEN

Sara listened to the wind howling. The rain had moved on and in its place, a chilly breeze pushed against the side of the house, rattling windows and a piece of loose siding on the third floor. Normally, the sound was nothing more than an annoying reminder that the place needed aesthetic repairs. Now, the continuous thumping reminded her of someone knocking repeatedly. It was unnerving, made her feel like a persistent intruder wanted inside.

She poured coffee in six large mugs, along with hot chocolate in three smaller ones for Lacey, Callie, and Jacob. Everyone had moved down to the basement where Sara had a pool table, several vintage arcade games, and plenty of books and movies for entertainment. It was safer down there, away from windows and doors. With no need to get home immediately, Randall and Mary had decided to stay for a while, at least until Barker reported in with something new.

Mary's husband Jim was in Florida for a conference; Randall's wife and son, Alice and Jesse, had called to check in—they were having fun on their trip and Randall had made no mention of his current situation.

Sara added containers full of cream and sugar to the tray, marshmallows for the kids, and was ready to head downstairs when her cell rang. She checked her caller ID and held her breath with the prospect of good news. "Hey, Barker," she answered.

"Sara, where are you?"

"At home, why?"

"Everything okay there?"

His tone was harried and concerned. It worried her. "What's going on?"

"You still got your buddies there? House locked down and all that?"

"Yeah. Did you find something?" Barker sounded like he was running. "Are you chasing somebody?"

"No, heading down the tarmac. FBI authorized a flight. Morrow and I will be there as soon as we can."

"Why? What happened?"

"Patty and Shelley are there. They landed in Bristol a couple of hours ago."

Sara dropped a spoon and it clanged against the metal tray. She jumped, spooked by the crash. "Are you sure?" The spoon landed on the floor, bounced, and disappeared under the stove.

"Visual ID, that's all we have, but it has to be

them. The pilots of a private flight out of Bend confirmed they carried two women matching the description."

Sara didn't want to believe it. *Refused* to believe it. "Anybody could match the description of a blonde and a brunette traveling together."

"Not when one of them only has one eye. It's Shelley, Sara. You know it and I know it."

Sara leaned against the countertop. Knees weak and shaking. She slid to the floor before she fell. "What do we do?" Her words cracked and crumbled out of her mouth. "How is this happening again, Barker?" She was strong—she'd survived both of these women already—but this was too much.

"Our best plan of—what? Hang on, Sara." She listened to him talk to someone nearby and heard the loud, sheer roar of plane engines. When he came back, he shouted, "Sorry, that was Morrow. We're sticking to the original plan, okay? Stay there, hunker down, and make sure everything is armed. He's not putting anyone on the ground on your property, but he'll have overhead surveillance and grab them on the way in."

Frantic, Sara got up to her knees. "Tell him to get people here now, Barker. I don't care what kind of idiotic plan he's got going on. I want protection. I want people here, in my house."

Again, he spoke to someone with him, "Yeah, one sec, I'll be right there," then said to Sara, "I've tried— by God, I've *tried*, but you gotta know this cat to understand he does things one way only: his and his alone. Whatever will bring him the most pats on the back. As much as I hate to say it, I'm just along for the ride. It's not the best plan by any stretch of the imagination, but I can see where he's trying to go with it. Like I told you earlier, he thinks that with boots on the ground, there's a high chance a bullet will find its way into her skull, and he wants her alive. She'll be a goldmine if he can get her into cuffs instead of a body bag."

"I don't care what *he* wants, Barker. It's *my* family." Sara felt weak, lightheaded. "You're coming, right? How soon can you be here?"

The roar of the engines quieted as he entered the hull of the plane. "Five hours, tops."

"Oh my God, Barker, if she landed at the Tri-Cities airport two hours ago, she could be sitting on my front porch already."

"Planes only go so fast. We're doing the best we can, all right? Make sure all your buttons are pushed and doors are locked, stay away from the windows, and hang on. Morrow already has people moving into position. You'll be fine, and more than likely, you won't even know they've been captured until you get another phone call from me. Okay? Tell me that's okay, Sara."

"Okay," she said, slowly climbing to her feet. "Just hurry. Please."

Down in the basement, the look on her face gave everything away.

"Sara?" Teddy said, getting up from his chair. He held a pool cue in one hand and a beer in another. "What's wrong?"

Her hands vibrated as she sat the tray of coffee and hot chocolate down on the bar. "Barker called."

"What did he say?"

She put on a fake smile and waited until her children had swarmed around her, laughing and grabbing their cocoa. They dumped marshmallows into their mugs by the handful and scampered away. She didn't have the strength, nor the heart, to tell them not to spill it on the carpet. With two women on their way to murder her, what difference did it make if there were a few chocolate stains on the carpet? She said, "They're already here."

"Who's here?" Randall asked. "The FBI?"

"No… Shelley and Patty."

Teddy slung his pool stick onto the green felt. Balls scattered. "Are you serious?"

Sara nodded and was unable to contain herself any longer. Tears flowed. Shoulders shook. She buried her face in her hands.

Miss Willow, Irina, and Mary came to her, stroking Sara's hair, rubbing her back and pulling her in for hugs. Teddy and Randall stood by, watching, unsure of where to put their hands, or their beers. The kids cautiously stepped over and asked Uncle Teddy what was wrong with their mother. "Your mom got some bad news, guys, just go back to Pac-Man for a bit."

Minutes later, the adults stood in stunned silence, waiting to hear the rest of Sara's news once she was able to compose herself. She wiped her nose with a bar napkin and handed out the coffee. No one seemed like they wanted to take the mugs, but she needed something to keep her hands occupied. "Barker said they took a private flight and he had confirmation from two pilots that they were at Tri-Cities approximately two hours ago."

Mary said, "That's it?"

"Yep." Sara dropped a sugar cube into her coffee. Then another, and finally a third. She never sweetened her coffee. It seemed that with each *plop* of a sugar cube, as it sank to the bottom and melted, a tiny bit of rage released. It felt good to destroy something. "That's it. The pilots confirmed a brunette woman matching Patty's description, and obviously, who's going to miss a disfigured, one-eyed creature like Shelley Sergeant, huh?"

Randall moved over to the bar and leaned down, resting his massive frame on his elbows, cradling the mug. "Then I guess that means it's killing time."

Mary shushed him and lowered her voice. "Not in front of the kids."

He nodded. "Right, sorry. So I take it you don't have any weapons in the house, do you?"

Sara said no and asked Miss Willow if she wouldn't mind shuffling the kids out of the room again. Poor things had been moved around the house all day like she was rearranging furniture, but they didn't need to be involved, or corrupted, by yet another instance like this. They were strong, and durable, but how much more could they handle in their young lives before trauma set in, before irreparable damage scarred them? Worse yet, what if their harrowing childhoods led them to lives like Patty and Shelley's?

Once they were gone from the room—with Irina volunteering to help—Sara explained Morrow's plan again, what she knew of it from Barker, and then added, "I mean, *my God*, how far do we have to go to live a peaceful life, huh? I'm seriously asking. Can anyone answer that question for me? Where, where, *where?*"

Mary pushed her coffee to the side and leaned down beside Randall. She was nearly a third of his size, but she spoke with such conviction and authority that she filled the room as much as he did. Sara liked her for that. It reminded her of the old days back at LightPulse, when she was a Vice President and could take over a meeting simply by stepping through the door. Mary said, "Sara, it might sound like a good plan on paper—right here, right now—but let me tell you this: if that agent wants her for information, if he wants to dig around in her brain for all these contact points she's got around the world, and all the dirt she knows about them…she's not going away forever."

"Why? What does that mean?"

"She'll cut a deal," Randall added. "The Sergeant woman might go back to the big house out in Oregon; they'll tack a few years onto her sentence and who knows when she'll get out. Maybe ten years, maybe never. But, this Kellog lady, she's got something they want, and if they manage to catch her, it won't take her long to find out that she can bargain herself into freedom in a hurry. These days, information moves mountains *and* governments."

"So what're you suggesting? That they'll be free in

a few years and this will happen all over again?"

"Can't say for certain, but people like these two, when they've got murder on their minds, it ain't likely that they'll just roll over and forget about it."

"And we'll never be able to get far enough away, will we?"

"Sara," Teddy said, "I know people. Dad knows people. Hell, you know Irina's whole damn family is tied to the Russian mob. We can get you a new identity. Papers, passports, driver's licenses, whatever you need, whatever the kids need. I'd hate to see you disappear because we think of you as family, and it'd be like me telling a sister to vanish, but I'd rather be confident that you were out there alive than six feet under because the FBI wants to know what moves the black markets in...in Laos or Shanghai, or whatever."

Sara reached into the cabinet below the bar and pulled out a bottle of Jack Daniels. "Anybody else?" Three arms went into the air. Sara added whiskey to each of their mugs, then took a long pull straight from the bottle before returning it to its rightful spot. "I'm not running, Teddy. Not if I don't have to."

"It makes sense."

"And leave my family behind? What about my parents?"

"It'll be worse if you and the kids are dead!"

"I'm sick of this shit. There has to be another way. Randall? Mary? Any ideas?"

Randall stood up straight and took a swig of the whiskey-laced coffee. He cleared his throat. "We were, uh, we were tossing some ideas around while you were upstairs."

"Like what?"

Mary said, "Before he gets riled up and excited about this, let me just say that I'm not the biggest fan of it. But, I agree with him, somewhat, even if it goes against everything we're standing here telling you."

Teddy agreed. "If we can't get you to disappear, which to me is the wisest choice, then…yeah, I'm on board with what Randall came up with."

"Tell me."

Randall pulled a stool out from the bar and sat down. He looked from Mary to Teddy and back again, then took a deep breath. "Okay, here goes, but before you tell me how mental this is, hear me out."

SIXTEEN

Teddy tried to reassure Irina as she stood in the doorway, crying, begging him not to go. "I'll be with Randall the whole way," he said. "He lives right over there in that old house. See it? Where the lights are on?"

Irina nodded, sniffling. "If anything happens to you—"

"It won't. I promise."

"You don't know that. You *can't* promise."

"Randall knows these hills better than the back of his hand. We'll be gone twenty minutes, tops, and then I'll come right back here to you."

"If you're not back in twenty, I'm coming to look for you, and I don't care who might be out there."

Teddy opened his mouth to counter her, but changed his mind. There was no use in arguing. As the granddaughter of Ivan, a former Russian mob boss, her determination and tenacity were just a couple of her admirable qualities, except for when they dissolved into bullheadedness and made situations challenging. He wiped a tear away with his thumb and kissed her cheek. "See you in a few, sweetheart."

Irina forced a smile.

Randall stood at the edge of the covered porch out back, waiting on him. He said, "Ready?"

"Yep, let's go."

"You don't have to come with me if you don't want to, especially if *she* don't want you to. I appreciate the offer, T-bird, but c'mon...y'all just got hitched."

Teddy leaned in and motioned for Randall to keep his voice down. "Don't give her any ideas, dude. It's the best plan and we all know it." He looked back over his shoulder at Irina and offered one last wave. Sara came to the doorway and told them to hurry.

Randall clapped Teddy on the back. "Okay, then. Stay close, stay low, and if you spot anything, even if a damn raccoon catches your eye, you point it out. God knows where those two heathens are by now—they could be sitting up there on the hill, scoping us with a thermal cam or night-vision goggles already, and we have to act like it, got me?"

"Roger that." Teddy followed Randall down the steps and into the last light of dusk. With the weather having passed by, leaving a smattering of clouds, what remained of the setting sun gave them a clean line of sight to their objective, Randall's house, but it also exposed them as targets. They chose to go on foot, rather than taking one of the cars, because they could move with more stealth once they made it to the trees surrounding the property.

Their plan was simple. A quick sprint to Randall's house to stock up on weapons and ammunition, then hunker down in Sara's home until some sign of Shelley and Patty appeared on Sara's monitoring system. There was no guarantee, but it had to happen. It was the only logical choice. Patty hadn't broken Shelley out of prison and flown across the entire United States, then landed at the closest commercial airport on a whim. Traveling, no matter the source of movement, was risky and dangerous. No, they were coming here. They were coming for a purpose.

Once the two invaders were spotted, Mary would take Sara, her children, and Miss Willow in Sara's oversized Suburban and get down the long driveway as rapidly as possible. Since Mary was trained in all styles of tactical driving and evasive maneuvers, she would be the one to get them to safety.

Teddy went over Randall's plan in his mind. Randall's hope was that the sudden escape would take Patty and Shelley by surprise. If they were dumb enough to give chase on foot, all the better. If they were smart enough to retreat, well, by then Randall would have a bead on their location. Two rapid shots from his perch on the third floor—dropping them both—and it would be game over, no matter what option they chose.

With Sara's connections, Mary's history, Randall's decorated service, and the fact that one enemy was an escaped convict and the other was a known international terrorist, Randall had said he was okay with the possibility that he might face legal action. So be it.

He'd admitted that was partly his burden—the inability to let injustice have its way with the world. He had his own family to worry about, he'd said, and in fact, he'd done dumber things in the recent past. But if he were incapable or didn't have the same level of training, he'd pray that someone would do the same for *his* family.

Teddy was glad this mighty monster was on their side. He hunched over and picked up his pace. All they had to do was make it to Randall's house, unarmed, without dying.

Sure. No problem.

Up at the fence, in the only gated doorway other than the driveway entrance, where the well-worn hiking trails led into the woods, Teddy entered Sara's PIN and they slipped through when the door swung open. He said to Randall, "Jesus, she really needs to set up a different code. She's used the same one for years.

186

Remind me to bug her about that when we get back, okay?"

"Will do, T-bird. Now keep your head down before you get it shot off."

They scrambled up the hillside until they reached the thin forest and then broke into sporadic bursts of speed, moving from birch, to maple, to oak.

They had gone close to ten acres away from Sara's home before Randall dropped to the ground and pulled Teddy with him in the process. Thankfully, due to the recent rain, the leaves were moist and didn't make too much noise as they landed and scuttled up behind a fallen oak trunk.

Teddy managed to get, "What is it—" out of his mouth before he felt Randall's bear paw across his lips, silencing him.

Randall held up two fingers, pointed at his eyes, and then further up the hillside. He mouthed, "Two," and used his fingers to pantomime a walking motion.

Teddy mouthed back, "Is it them?"

Randall shrugged, put his fingers to his lips, and lifted his head over the trunk just enough to peek with one eye.

Teddy did the same. Far above their position, he spied two black-clad figures darting from tree to tree, moving in a northerly direction, and he assumed that they hadn't been spotted.

But were Shelley and Patty here already? Before the sun went down completely? It didn't make sense. Would they risk it?

If they were coming, and every known fact indicated that they were, he'd assumed they would wait until darkness fell. A new moon, along with sporadic cloud cover, would provide a perfect nighttime approach.

So why risk it now in the waning light of dusk?

Randall motioned for Teddy to stay low and nudged himself up again. He was intently focused while the two figures move through the forest. "That ain't them," he whispered seconds later, patting Teddy on the shoulder. "That's my reinforcements."

"Who?"

"A couple of my buddies I called up while you were in the pisser earlier. Two coon hunters named Dale and Harold, here to keep an eye on the perimeter. They're practically invisible in these woods."

"Yeah, but *you* saw them."

"That's because I know what to look for." Randall put his thumb and forefinger in his mouth and let loose with a shrill, three-note whistle. From somewhere north of their position, closer to Sara's house, came a reply. He grabbed Teddy's arm and pulled him to his feet. "Let's go."

"That's it?"

"They know what to do."

Randall moved, deftly, in a brisk jog, hopping over fallen trees and ducking around low-hanging limbs. Teddy managed to keep up, but not without some complaints over the pace or the branches that kept poking him in the eyes. Once they were near the road, Randall dropped into a cluster of rhododendrons and crawled forward.

Teddy followed. "What're we doing?"

Randall pointed, indicating the cow pasture on the opposite side. "Wide open space over there. Just making sure we're in the clear. It's another three minutes down to my front porch if we hurry, and then less than ten back before your wife comes after us."

"She won't," Teddy said. "She talks a bigger game than she plays. Although…"

"What's that?"

"Her grandpa was in the Russian mafia for a while, and I know that old dude's got connections and family all up and down the east coast. I bet if she made a couple of phone calls, we could have some of them here running backup, too. Would that make sense? Your redneck buddies and my Kremlin relatives hanging out in the woods together?"

Randall chuckled and pushed up to a crouch. "I wish we had the time for it. That'd make a helluva show on HBO. Let's move." Down the embankment he went, Teddy following, until he reached the blacktop. "Run," he said, without waiting. Arms pumping, one leg in front of the other.

Teddy knew the distance to Randall's front porch, from this point, would be less than a quarter of a mile away. Short enough, but it seemed like it was on the other side of the planet. A single light illuminated a room on the second floor of the farmhouse. It was a small thing, but Teddy thanked God for it, because the glow provided a warm beacon in the darkening night.

Teddy jogged easily beside Randall, keeping up with the taller man's long strides.

"Run much?" Randall asked, a slightly winded huff in his voice. He stayed in shape with free weights and hiking through the mountains, hunting and finding the best fishing spots. There was never any reason to be at a higher speed than amble.

"Ten miles every day," Teddy said. "Six minute miles at a normal cruising speed."

"Then we know who we're sending if someone has to run after the cops, huh?"

"Whatever it takes, man."

Directly in front of them, the trees in the bend lit

up from the lights of an approaching car.

"Shit," Randall said. He looked around for a spot to hide.

"Who's that?"

"No idea, but just in case. There!" He pointed to a long, blue trough like the one he'd seen near Sara's barn. "Duck and cover, T-bird."

Randall dropped off the side of the embankment and climbed over the fence with Teddy following close behind.

The earth surrounding the trough was deep, thick mud, made that way by the herd of cattle tromping through twice daily during feeding times. He'd been through worse, and had hidden in worse things during his time as a sniper, but flopping down in mud and cow shit was never an option he'd choose on purpose. Grabbing the trough, he said, "Help me with this. Get that end."

"Whoa, what're we doing?"

"Hiding. Gotta hurry. C'mon now, grab that end."

"Under this?"

"Teddy, damn it, pull your end."

Over Randall's left shoulder, Teddy saw the headlights coming into view, watching as the cone of light swept over the trees, past the farmhouse, and through the field. They'd be visible in five…four…three…

Teddy said, "Yep, got it," and leaned with all his weight against the large, metal frame, which was just enough to help Randall topple the trough. They fell face first into the gunk as it landed with a splatter, sending mud and cow pies squishing out in all directions.

Randall listened to the approaching car and watched it through a rusted hole in the trough's bottom. He was certain they hadn't been spotted in the headlights—and he wondered if he'd overreacted—but given the current situation, being too careful wasn't possible.

Not that he knew every car in town, but he recognized most of the cars that came through this route on a regular basis. That was one of the quirks of living in a small town; a man could set his watch by the neighbors' schedules.

But this one—and it was hard to tell in the low light—this wasn't a car he recognized. Dark in color, a sedan, and maybe a newer model. Could be somebody down the road, maybe Tom Hammerly or Carter Conley, had traded in for a new one, but—

"Who is it?" Teddy whispered. "Anybody you know?"

"Can't tell. Probably nobody. Just somebody

passing through."

It could've easily been true if the car hadn't stopped thirty feet away, idling in the middle of the road.

Teddy held his breath as the engine shut off.

SEVENTEEN

Patty stopped the blue rental car in the middle of the road. "That's it right there," she said, pointing up through the field. "Sara thinks she's got her castle guarded, but everything has a way in and a way out."

Shelley craned her head around to see out of her good eye. "That's a lot of ground to cover, huh? Look at that fence…is that the one with the lasers?"

Patty shut off the engine and opened the door. "Let me show you what we're up against."

"Hey, are you nuts? Get back in the car. What if she's got cameras down here?"

"Then she'll know we're coming, but not when or where, and I like that idea."

"Uh, hello? Police? Guns?"

Patty leaned back inside the vehicle. "Would you trust me? Jesus. It's taken care of."

"How?"

Patty rolled her eyes. "Extraction point, one point three miles from here. We're in, we're out, and they'll never find us, not running through these woods."

"What if she's calling the cops right now?"

"Then we listen for sirens, Shelley. Get out of the

damn car so I can show you what you need to see and then we'll go."

"Fine." Shelley climbed out and closed the door. She walked around the front of the car and hid her nose in a sleeve. "You think cows know they stink so much?"

Patty chuckled and put her arm around Shelley's waist. She pulled her close and felt her body's warmth against the cool spring air. "Okay, here's what we're up against." She explained the lasers, the heat-detecting cameras, the motion sensors, the weight triggers in the driveway, the depths to which the concrete ran under the fence, and everything else that she knew about Sara Winthrop's nearly impenetrable security system. "Finally," she said, planting a kiss on Shelley's cheek, "we don't have to worry about any cameras right here, because the four guarding the south side are all focused on the entrance since that's the primary access point. At most, she might've seen the car's headlights go by on the main road, but from right here, we could sit and stare at her house all night."

The corner of Shelley's mouth turned up. "You little shit. You had me freaking out."

"And you gotta start trusting the pro, sweetheart. Money leads to information. Always has and always will. Learn that first thing and the roads ahead are always smoother. We don't survive in this business by being brain-dead morons."

"Like Bobby?"

"Exactly, and to be perfectly honest, I'm surprised somebody hadn't offed him before us."

"So what's the plan from here?"

Patty smiled and stroked Shelley's hair. "Shock and awe sound good to you?"

***

Patty drove them to a spot two miles from Sara's home. It was a small garbage station bordered by a chain link fence roughly eight feet high. Normally locked, the night attendant had graciously accepted the hundred-dollar bill, weeks ago, to leave the sliding gate open on the prearranged date.

Shelley hopped out, rolled the gate to the side, and then closed it again as Patty hid the car behind the largest green disposal unit. It was roughly the size of a boxcar and hid the rented sedan well.

Even in the cool air of a spring night, the smell was putrid, and Patty couldn't imagine what it was like in the middle of summer. Spoiled milk, rotting meat, and God knows what else rampaged through her nostrils. She tried to breathe through her mouth as they stripped down. "Everything off," she said. "The closer you can get it to your skin, the better these heat-dispensing suits work."

Beside her, Shelley shivered in the cold. Patty let her eyes trail over her partner's body, admiring it, feeling the pull of longing, and wished they had more time and a spot that didn't melt flowers with its smell. Shelley's figure was nearly flawless, marred only by the scars, evidence that she had survived a brutal attack.

Patty chuckled and shook her head.

"What?" Shelley said.

"Nothing."

"Tell me."

"All those scars make you more attractive."

"Whatever."

"It's the truth. It's like you went through battle and came out a beast on the other side. I love it."

"Freak." Shelley grinned, turned around and then lifted her hair. "Here, zip me and then I'll get yours."

When they were fully dressed in their suits, nothing but their eyes showing, Patty handed over a set of night vision goggles and a sub-compact 9mm Glock that was small, powerful, and easily transportable over mildly challenging terrain. She gave Shelley two more spare magazines. "Are you ready?" she asked.

"That's it?" Shelley replied, glancing down at the

smaller Glock in one hand and the magazines in another.

"Honey, if you need more than that, we'll need to rethink this partnership." Patty tucked her Heckler & Koch 9mm into an interior pocket.

"Okay, then I guess I'm ready."

"Good, let's go."

"We're leaving the car here? What about all this extra stuff?"

Patty checked her watch. "In seven minutes and forty-five seconds, it'll be gone. Two hours from now, they'll find it burning at a rest stop thirty miles south from here. The rest of our gear will be delivered to us as soon as we're ready to disappear. Any more questions?"

"Do you always think of everything?"

"I'm still alive, aren't I?"

They ran through the gate, down the road for an eighth of a mile, and then right and up into the wooded hillside. The night vision goggles made the jaunt easier to duck under clawing limbs, hop over fallen trees, and avoid twisting ankles on loose rocks. Down into a miniature valley and then up the ridgeline to the north, through the rolling hills, between springtime trees with little canopy overhead. No moon, guided by starlight and the hazy green view from their goggles.

Patty was in excellent shape, but Shelley struggled to keep up. Behind her, the young woman huffed and sucked wind, trying to maintain the pace but falling behind. "You okay?" Patty asked.

"No," was the breathless reply.

"Didn't you exercise in prison?"

"I spent that hour in the yard each day trying to stay alive, so excuse me if there wasn't time to run a few laps."

Patty stopped at the top of the ridge, giving Shelley time to catch up. "And whose fault is that?"

"Mine?" Shelley flopped onto a moss-covered log.

"Sara Winthrop's, and don't you forget it. Look at me. Look." Shelley turned her head up. "Find whatever fire you've got in your heart and use it. All that anger and rage is fuel. Do you understand me?"

"Yeah."

"Then get up. Let's go."

Running.

Running.

They spooked a small herd of deer that had bedded down for the night and kept going. Out here, so far away from another home or the lights of city streets, no one would notice panicked wildlife scattering to escape the human intruders.

Up ahead, where the trees thinned, they reached a fencerow that opened into an empty hayfield. "Here we are," Patty said, ducking low and crouching next to a large maple. "That's the back side of her land, right there. Look past that fence post at your one o'clock—see her house over there where the lights are?"

"Yeah."

"That's where we're going, but first, let me show you something." She dropped to her stomach and army-crawled over to the fence. She looked back over her shoulder and motioned for Shelley to join her, and once they were side by side, lying on the cool forest floor, Patty pointed up to the top of the post. "Can you see it?"

"See what?"

"Look right up at the top."

"It's dark and I have one eye, damn it. Just tell me what I'm looking for."

"The laser, remember? That's what this is for." Patty removed a device from her backpack and showed Shelley. "Bobby had to get this thing into the country all the way from Moscow. Mirrors on either end—right here and here—telescoping feature so it can go from post to post, and then these clamps. It breaks the beam without triggering the alarm." Patty pulled at either end, stretching it out, and then twisted a knob to secure the two pieces in place. She got to her knees and then hesitated.

Shelley asked, "Are you sure it'll work? I mean, won't it break the beam while you're trying to get it in place?"

"They told me there's a half-second delay to prevent things like those deer back there from setting it off every time one jumps across the fence. Somehow, it measures body temperature too, you know, so if a squirrel is sitting up there, that won't trigger it either."

"*They?*"

"The security company that installed it."

"Somebody told you?"

"Everybody has a price. I told you that already." Swiftly, Patty jumped to her feet, thrust the device forward, felt the clamps snap securely around the top of the post, and looked closely at the red dot shining back on itself. She waited, watching Sara's place for any sign of movement, any indication that a warning had been triggered. No floodlights came on, no wailing alarms sounded, and everything appeared quiet at the farmhouse acres away. She sighed with relief. "So far, so good."

"Now what?" Shelley asked.

"Now we wait."

"Why?"

Patty checked her watch. "Our two decoys should've been here already. Damn it, I knew I should've—" A branch snapped nearby. Patty pulled her handgun free and aimed. Shelley spun from her prone position on the ground and did the same. "Who's there?" Patty whispered.

A hushed voice came from behind a small patch of briars. "Y'all put them guns down."

Patty felt her stomach churn. She didn't recognize the voice. She increased the pressure under her trigger finger, ready to pull. She hesitated just long enough for the voice to say, "You the one they call Patty?"

"Yeah," she said. "Come out in the open so we can see you."

"All right then. It's just the two of us. No shootin', you hear?" Two large men lurched from behind the briars, hands up, showing they were safe...but maybe not unarmed.

Patty inched back, never pointing her barrel away from the closest one's chest. "What happened to Tess and Laura?"

They both wavered, and Patty noticed.

"They sent us instead. Got scared."

"And who're you?"

"Husbands. I'm Dale and this is Harold."

The one in the rear lifted his hand and said, "Ma'am."

Patty wasn't comfortable with this development. Not at all. Sure, plans change, they go astray, and you have to be prepared to make snap decisions, but this was inexcusable and she hated it when things got out of control. The two women she'd recruited at a local bar, months ago, had been strung out on meth and who knows how many other chemicals. Patty shook her head. She should've known better. All she needed was a couple of distractions, and to put her trust in two crackheads like Tess and Laura to show up on the right night at the right time, for a big payday, had probably been too much to ask.

"Are you armed?" she asked.

Dale shook his head. "No, ma'am. They said *you'd* be though, and we can see that."

"Two bullets, boys, and that's all it'll take. The scavengers will be plucking out your eyeballs before anyone finds you."

"Right as rain, ma'am. Whatever you need. And speaking of which, what the hell are we doing here?"

"They didn't tell you?"

The one called Harold lifted his broad shoulders to his ears and let them drop. "Said something about meeting this here lady on the back side of the

Winthrop farm right about now. Said you'd tell us what to do."

Patty took a deep breath. It didn't feel right, but she couldn't think of a test to challenge them. Were these two goobers smart enough to deceive her, or were they dumb enough to show up for their wives, no matter what the women asked of them? "You have no idea why you're here?"

"All we know is, there's supposed to be some kind of reward."

Patty glanced over at Shelley. The young woman inhaled heavily through her nostrils, waiting, watching. Patty asked her, "You trust these two?"

"Maybe. Ask them where you met their wives."

Patty saw the two men exchange a fleeting look. "Well?"

"Down at Pickle's Bar and Grill."

The tension in her shoulders relaxed, but only slightly. He was right, yet it still didn't change the fact that she wasn't comfortable with the last minute switch. She said, "Okay. But I'm not happy about this so I'm cutting the payout in half, got it?"

"Yes, ma'am."

She took a step to the side and pointed at the fence section with the blocked laser. "Simple deal, guys. All we need you to do is cross the fence and run toward the Winthrop house. We need you to trigger the motion sensors and the thermal imaging cameras."

"That's it?"

"Yes."

"And what're you gonna be doing?"

Patty stepped an inch closer and aimed between Harold's eyes. "Ask me another question."

"Nah, I think I'm good."

"You run toward her house, then break off and get the hell out of there the second you see any indication that they're aware you're coming. Floodlights, alarms, whatever."

"That's it?"

"Yep."

Harold and Dale shrugged and started toward the fence. They approached too close to Patty. It made her wary. She put her finger back on the trigger.

Something had been tingling in the back of her mind. Something was off that she couldn't place...and then what Dale had said crossed her mind: "*You the one they call Patty?*"

She hadn't told Tess and Laura her name.

Dale took a darting step in her direction as she raised her gun.

EIGHTEEN

Randall and Teddy retraced their steps carrying flashlights, several handguns, a bag full of MREs just in case they had to hunker down and ride out an assault, and a Barrett .50 caliber sniper rifle that Randall called "Goliath."

They ran as fast as they could go, carrying their cargo back up the road, because Randall had managed to overhear the two women talking once they'd gotten out of the car. The words, "Shock and awe sound good to you?" had sent chills down his spine, and once the women were gone, he and Teddy had debated on whether they should go back to the house or keep going.

In the end, they decided that the better option was arming themselves. Either they would get back in time to defend the property, or they would encounter the two women somewhere along the fence, trying to find a way inside, and Randall would easily be able to take them down with two wounding shots.

When they reached the edge of Sara's land, Randall backed up against the brick corner pillar and waited on Teddy to sidle up beside him. "Okay," he said, "stay behind me, stay smart, and stay quiet. Who knows where they went from here, but I can guaran-damn-tee you that it wasn't far, and they'll be close enough to get back on foot."

"How do you know that?"

"Because it's what I would do. If that Patty lady has had any kind of tactical training, she'll know that they'll be less visible on foot, so I'd bet my left nut they're coming in from the eastern side where the woods are the thickest. I'm hoping that Dale and Harold are in a position to keep an eye on them."

"Cool, yeah, but how will we know where your buddies are?"

"You know what a whippoorwill sounds like?"

"That's like a cousin to a Greyhound, right?"

Randall chuckled and shook his head. "Bird. Not a dog." He pursed his lips and offered a soft, lilting demonstration, enough for Teddy to hear and comprehend.

"Got it."

"You hear that, you'll know Dale and Harold have eyes on us. Drop and wait. One of them will come tell us where our two lady friends are hiding."

"Any last words of advice?"

"Yeah, keep your ass low, and your head lower. Time to rock, T-bird."

For a big man, Randall moved nimbly, gliding effortlessly back through the forest. He followed his own advice, keeping a low profile, moving from tree to tree and bush to bush in rapid spurts. If they'd had the time, he would've preferred a slower, more concealed approach, but that luxury wasn't possible. He recalled the days and weeks he'd spent in the jungles of South America or the deserts of the Middle East, remaining invisible to the enemy while he positioned himself for the perfect shot. Rain, heat, bugs, snakes, or nearly collapsing from exhaustion were never an issue. One shot, one kill, do it better next time.

He missed those days.

This was different.

How would Alice feel if she knew he was risking his life to protect strangers?

Angry, obviously. He could hear her now… "What about Jesse? What about me? You have a goddamn family to think about, Randall. I thought you were done with stupid shit like this. After that game you played? Are you serious? We didn't think you were coming back to us. Not ever."

He understood what it must be like for her, but did she understand his need to defend against the bad guys, regardless of who they were, where they were, or what their motives might be? She never had. Not for as long as they'd been together. Yeah, participating in that damn game had been the dumbest decision he'd ever made, but he was alive, and that was all that mattered. He supposed that fighting back against the bad guys was a result of getting picked on so much growing up. He knew what it was like to be on that side of things, so whenever an opportunity arose to take down one of the bastards that was making someone else's life a living hell, then yes, sir, where should I sign?

Randall paused beside another brick pillar. Teddy flopped down beside him. Sweat poured from the little man's forehead, and Randall assumed it was from the nerves, because he wasn't even breathing hard. Randall asked, "You good?"

"You ever have to take a piss when you get nervous that's so bad, you can actually feel it sloshing around?"

"Nervous? *Pfft.* Never heard the word before."

"Figures. Why'd we stop?"

Randall flicked his chin northward. "About a hundred yards up. You see those two black masses on the ground?" Teddy peered around the edge. Randall grabbed his shoulder and pulled him back immediately. "Don't get your damn head shot off, T-bird. Just poke it out there a little."

Teddy did as he was instructed. "It's hard to tell, but I think so, yeah. What is it?"

"Dunno, but they weren't there when we came through the first time."

"Is it your buddies?"

"Let's find out." Randall puckered his lips and whistled like a whippoorwill. The three-tone chime went unanswered. He did it again, and still, no response. He grunted and handed Teddy his rucksack. "Take this a sec, would you? I'm gonna check it out with the scope."

He eased Goliath around the pillar and lowered his eye to the .50 cal's scope, then pushed the button to turn on night vision. He focused, took a deep breath, and saw what he feared had happened. "No," he said.

"What?"

"Move, move." Randall was on his feet and running before Teddy had a chance to ask why. Concern, not panic, gripped his lungs as he traversed the hillside while trying to maintain their cover.

As he approached the two black lumps, he cursed and dropped to the ground, made himself as flat as possible. Teddy joined him. They were too open, too exposed, and it wasn't smart, but as far as he could tell, they were too late.

Patty and Shelley had done their damage and were inside the property.

He army-crawled over and saw Dale's lifeless eyes staring up at the stars. Harold's, too. Both men, good men, were gone, the bullet holes in their foreheads a clear stamp that they'd met their ends too soon. "Son of a goddamn bitch," Randall said.

"Is that…"

"Yeah."

"Oh, God…I'm sorry…oh God, that sucks."

"We need to move." He felt Dale's cheek. "Still warm."

"Shouldn't we call the cops?"

"Unless you want to find everyone in the house like this, let's go. We'll make sad faces later. On second thought, can you talk and run?"

"Yeah."

"Then call the house. Let Sara know those two are on the farm already and we're coming."

"Got it."

Randall paused at the fence and examined the device the intruders had used to block the laser. Not too sophisticated, but high tech enough that the Kellog woman had to have some qualified connections and a good bankroll.

Behind him, Teddy explained the situation to Sara,

then hung up. "She says they're ready. They'll be waiting for us at the door."

"Good. Now all we need to do is figure out which direction they went."

He surveyed the terrain, trying to decide which would be the safest way to get back to the others. From here, it was an open expanse of three acres straight across a hayfield to Sara's farmhouse.

They wouldn't have gone that way. Sure, they could've crossed it with ease—shortest distance between two points and all that—but even with the minimum ambient light, they would've been too out in the open. He assumed Patty was smarter than that. It was too revealing. She knew better. So, that meant they'd crossed, stayed close to the fence, and would approach from a more concealed route.

He put Goliath up to his shoulder and used the scope to examine the house. Everything appeared to be calm and quiet over there. Which was strange, now that he thought about it, because he recalled Sara mentioning that there were thermal imaging cameras stationed around the perimeter. Had the two women disabled them?

Surely, if Sara had been watching the monitors like she was supposed to, she would've seen the four people in this location and raised an alarm.

Right? So what happened?

How would the two women have known where those cameras were?

Did they have inside information?

Too many questions, too little time.

He'd paused for too long, because Teddy said, "Randall?"

He didn't see a path through the field where light boots had trampled rain-soaked hay, so he guessed his assumptions were correct. "We're going straight across. Point A to Point B, T-bird. Shortest distance."

"That seems dangerous, man. Out in the open like that? Why?"

"We're going that way because *they* didn't."

Randall scrambled over the fence. Teddy followed.

It wasn't the most concealed route, but from the looks of the entry wounds in Dale and Harold, the two women were carrying close-range, small-caliber weapons. They would want to move swiftly, quietly, and unencumbered, so the risk of a long-range rifle was minimal.

If he had a proper bead on Patty Kellog's style, she would approach with stealth, given the fact that they'd gone through the trouble of interrupting the laser. She and Shelley would rely on her skills as an assassin, rather than punching through with brute force. Cutting straight across the field managed to be the smartest and dumbest decision he and Teddy could make.

Time trumped caution.

Randall pumped his legs. His rucksack swung wildly on his back. He gripped Goliath tightly in his left hand and pulled a .45 semi-automatic pistol free from the holster at his waist. His footsteps pounded the soggy field as hay stalks rubbed against his thighs, soaking his jeans. Teddy caught up and nearly overtook him, then slowed by a half step to match his pace.

He didn't know if Teddy was smart enough to not take the position as lead runner, or if he'd simply held up so they could go together. If it was the former, he'd likely saved himself from taking a bullet first. "Zig zag," he told Teddy. "Harder to hit."

Two hundred yards and closing. Randall kept his eyes trained on the house as they angled back and forth across the open field, expecting to feel metal slugs penetrating his side at any moment.

Or, in the event of a lucky shot, he'd take one in the side of the head and never know it. He didn't want to risk looking around—somehow, in doing so, it felt like he would be jinxing the whole thing. Take a peek, welcome an open hole in his chest. He kept his head low and signaled for Teddy to cut left.

Fifty yards from the farmhouse. Almost there. The

impending dread eased up slightly. They were close. "Right," he said, and angled north.

Teddy tracked him, took two steps, and then screamed in pain. At the same time, the sound of a gunshot echoed through the nearby hills.

Randall hunched over, turned, and watched as Teddy rolled, holding his shoulder. Teddy sprang back to his feet. Randall shouted, "You hit?"

"I'm okay. Go, go, go," Teddy said, pointing toward the house. "Grazed me."

They sprinted. As they dipped back and forth in a wild, angular pattern, Randall asked, "Where'd it come from?"

"Don't know. Behind, maybe."

Twenty yards away from the cover of Sara's home. Randall stopped, pivoted, and dropped to one knee. "Get inside."

"But—"

"Now, Teddy."

The two women could be anywhere. Randall lifted his .45 and before he squeezed the trigger, wet earth kicked up beside his leg. Too close. He fired once, twice, three times, the pops loud in his ears. He fired again, wildly. With acres and acres spread out in front of him, he was shooting blind.

Tool shed? Could they be in the tool shed? He

fired at it, again and again, unsure if he'd hit anything. At this distance and lack of light, he couldn't be sure.

Another plume of earth kicked up to his left, even closer than the other one. Three inches from his foot, if that.

Gotta go, chief. No use. Can't tell where it's coming from.

He fired off two more shots and scrambled toward the house. Teddy crouched at the side entrance, holding the door open, frantically waving for Randall to hurry.

"Come on!" Teddy shouted.

"Get in there. I'm coming."

"Hurry."

Randall leaped over an overturned wheelbarrow and skirted a flowerbed. Thirty feet from the house and closing. Long, great strides covering yards with each new step. Almost there, two more steps, and then close to the porch—

The pain wasn't as bad as he remembered. He'd been shot before, but never in his hamstring. It was more like a sledgehammer slamming into the back of his leg. A thick, dull ache, combined with a force that pitched him forward and sent him down to the ground, rolling, and then hobbling back to his feet.

He reached the steps. Wood splintered to his right, then again.

He climbed.

He prayed.

NINETEEN

From the side window of the old tool shed, Patty focused intently on Sara Winthrop's farmhouse. She waited patiently while Shelley paced back and forth, unable to stand in one place for more than five seconds. "Would you relax?" she said.

"I'm not nervous, I'm excited."

"That's fine, but Jesus, sit down before you make *me* nervous."

"Whatever." Shelley flopped down on a workbench, left leg bouncing like the needle of a sewing machine. "Can I pull the trigger?"

"What?" Patty turned to face her.

"You know, when we're ready. Let me do it."

Patty shook her head. "Sorry, hon, this one's mine. You can have all the rest, but Sara's got twenty years of messing with my brain to make up for."

Shelley stomped over to Patty and jammed a finger at the side of her own head. "I lost an eye, Patty. I'm a *monster* because of her."

Patty nodded slightly. "Yeah, there's that. Let me think about it."

"What're we gonna do first? What've you got in mind? I mean, we're here, shouldn't you tell me what your brilliant plan is?"

"Tic-Tac-Toe. Monopoly, maybe?"

"Be serious."

"You'll see." Patty returned her attention to the small window. The glass had broken out long ago, and aside from a few shards, she had a clear view into the cool night air. Down at the farmhouse, everything appeared to be normal. They'd reached her first planned destination unobserved, and now came the waiting. The two men that she and Shelley had killed troubled her. First, it meant that someone knew she and Shelley were coming. Back in Oregon, the police or the FBI had discovered where they'd gone and the information had leaked three thousand miles.

But, those two men weren't police or FBI. She'd checked for credentials and found nothing but two wallets, a can of Skoal, and some chewing tobacco. Maybe they weren't carrying identifications, but they were too far out of shape and too…country to be government stiffs.

Regardless, whoever they were, if those goons were Sara's first line of defense, patrolling the outer edges of her property, then she'd chosen poorly. However, it meant Sara was aware that she might be the target of a new attack.

First, Patty realized her plans would have to be altered. She'd had an elaborate scheme worked out wherein Sara would play yet another multi-level game, all in honor of Shelley. The babysitter would go first, then the children, and finally Sara, the idea being that she would be made to suffer through all of it, because the suffering would be infinitely worse than dying an easy death. She hated the idea of disappointing Shelley, but nothing could be done. Now there were too many unknown factors inside the Winthrop farmhouse.

Second, it meant that Sara was prepared for her and Shelley's arrival, which made the fact that no alarms had been raised yet all the more troubling. She couldn't figure it out. Maybe their equipment had worked as well as she'd hoped. They'd been invisible to the cameras; the laser hadn't alerted the security monitoring system; and so far, she saw no additional signs of law enforcement. Truly, it was strange all around.

Were the two men outside the boundary the only ones? Had they been placed there to maintain surveillance? The direction from which she and Shelley had entered was the most logical one—cover from the forest, closer to the house than other points on the compass—so it made sense that those men were in the area. Obviously they hadn't alerted anyone in the house before they approached.

It didn't make any goddamn sense. Was it a trap?

It had to be. If Sara knew she and Shelley were coming, then luring her in close enough to capture—or kill her—was the only remaining option. Otherwise, the place would be swarming with protection and they wouldn't have gotten within miles of the place.

Smart. Maybe.

Patty had the feeling they were being watched and scanned the interior of the tool shed for cameras. The place was clean. Based on the information she'd purchased, she already knew there wasn't one inside, but visual confirmation eased her sense of wariness.

Shelley said, "This isn't a 'need to know' thing, Patty. Tell me."

"Damn it, Shelley—I *don't* know, okay? Not anymore. Something doesn't feel right and I can't put a finger on what. I think they're pulling us into a trap and part of me wants to call it off. It's probably smarter for us to back out and come at her again some other time."

"What? No!"

"I'm serious. I say we walk. If you can smell the shit before you step in it, then it's time to take a different path." Patty could see the disappointment on the poor girl's face, but she hadn't made it this long in her line of work by giving in to pleading eyes.

Or eye, in Shelley's case.

No, it was best that they back out. Sara wasn't going anywhere. She would have to leave the house one day to shop for groceries, or take the kids to school, for anything, really, and they would strike then. Patty had been looking forward to taking care of business inside Sara's home where she thought she was safe and secure. Nothing would've been more satisfying than to watch the terror in her eyes as they swaggered through the front door unannounced. With the opportunity slipping away, she felt a bit of sadness in her chest, but decided that the disappointment was better than iron bars and a lumpy cot.

Shit. Time wasted. Money wasted. Eight months of prep, gone. Maybe now would be a good time for a vacation.

Well, after she had a west-coast friend eliminate her inside contact at the security company that installed Sara's system. Bill Chester, doting husband, father of three, subject to taking large bribes to flip some switches at a predetermined time, would need to be dead by morning.

Patty sighed, checked her watch, and felt two hands clamp around her throat.

Squeezing tightly, Shelley hissed, "That bitch dies

tonight, and you are *not* taking this away from me." She shoved Patty up against the wall. Rusted tools with rotting wooden handles—a tobacco hatchet, a saw, and a post-hole digger—rattled where they hung. The table Patty sat on tipped back and stopped at an odd angle.

Patty fought for her breath, feeling fingers contracting around her windpipe, clawing at Shelley's arms. She looked up into a single, determined eye. Spittle flew from her mouth as she managed to get her arms under Shelley's, and using a foot against the table for leverage, she brought her hands up. She shoved and broke the hold. Then, with the other foot, her boot went to Shelley's chest, kicking, thrusting as hard as she could, driving her back.

Shelley tripped on a shovel and went down.

Patty spun around and reached for her firearm, with full intention of putting a bullet through Shelley's forehead. She'd grown attached to the girl, but there was no room in her life for complications like that; retaliate against a wrong and move on. Shelley would die in the tool shed, and Patty would mourn for a pathetic second, then get on with her life. Sara would still be here and other opportunities for retribution would arise in the future.

Her fingers closed around the pistol grip. She heard Shelley trying to get to her feet behind her.

Movement outside caught her eye. Through the window, she saw two hunched figures sprinting across the field, toward the farmhouse. For a moment she thought she was seeing ghosts—Dale and Harold come back to life to warn Sara—then she realized these were two *different* men. One much larger, one much smaller. Who were these guys? Two more sentries that had been posted?

She aimed, leading her target, and fired.

The smaller one dropped, rolled, and sprang up to his feet. He ran, holding his shoulder.

Patty felt Shelley's arm around her neck, yanking her backward. She swung an elbow, driving it into soft ribs. Shelley grunted and went down. Patty hesitated, then drove the butt of her pistol into Shelley's temple.

Knocked out, her body flopped to the side.

Back to the window, seconds later, the small man had made it to the house. The larger one was on his knee, firing wildly.

She fired and missed. Fired again and missed another time. She watched as he focused his attention on the tool shed. Shots rang out. Wood splintered outside the walls.

She ducked until he stopped firing, risked a glance, and saw him sprinting through the yard, leaping a wheelbarrow. He moved so fast for his size.

Patty fired yet again and sent the large man to the ground. As he crawled, clutching his leg, she fired again and again, missing, watching him duck and cover his head. She fired until the magazine was empty and reached for another, but the delay was enough to permit their escape.

When she looked again, the last she saw of them was the larger man limping through the door as it swung closed behind him.

She cursed and pounded a fist on the table. She clenched her teeth.

Shelley.

The girl lay on the ground, unconscious, and when Patty nudged her with a boot, she stirred, groaning softly as she tried to sit up.

Patty pushed her back down, straddled her, and held the barrel of her firearm an inch away from the tip of Shelley's nose. She grabbed a handful of Shelley's hair and yanked hard, twisting and pulling her face closer. "Stupid asshole," she said. "You—you are a stupid asshole. Give me one reason why I shouldn't pull the trigger. Just one, because I am *this close* to dropping you right here. I'll do it. I *will* do it. Understand me?"

Shelley winced. Her nostrils flared. She eyed Patty and remained silent.

"Nothing? Huh? Nothing? You *want* me to do it, don't you?"

One heartbeat, two heartbeats, three heartbeats pounded inside Patty's skull. "I'll do it," she said, but she wasn't sure that she actually would, now that she held Shelley's pitiable life in her hands. One finger, one trigger, one second, and it would be over.

Patty felt the anger roiling in her stomach. She'd never hesitated before. She'd survived by being ruthless, so what was this? Why couldn't she do it? Why couldn't she rid herself of this troublesome...*gnat?*

Was it care? Was it feeling? Was it some godforsaken emotional attachment?

"Sorry," Shelley whimpered.

And that was enough.

Patty got up and pulled Shelley to her feet, by her hair—not coddling her, she didn't deserve it—but for now she'd keep her alive. "I know how badly you want this, but so help me God, if you ever, ever do anything like that again...finger, trigger, bullet. Dead, done, gone."

Shelley nodded and brushed Patty's hand away from her hair. "I...I couldn't control myself. I don't know where it came from."

"Use it on them, *not* me."

"I know."

"You have to learn to be in charge of yourself. You don't know shit about me. You don't know the things I've done. You don't know the things I'm capable of. I'm not some little tart in prison that you can push around. I'm not one of your weakling…victims. Do you understand that *I* am death?"

"Yes."

"Good. Now while you were out, two more armed men ran into the house. Who knows how many more are in there and what kind of arsenal they have. We don't know if we're trapped in here and there are fifty scopes on us right now, we don't know anything, Shelley, and the only thing I can guarantee is that"— she checked her watch—"in about six minutes, the entire security system is going down. So let me ask you something: are you ready to die for this tonight? Are you going to be that stupid, or do we walk and come back when we know what we're up against?"

Shelley shrugged.

"We survive by being smart. It's worked for me for twenty years."

"We can be smart and still do this."

"How, huh? Explain it to me."

Shelley nodded at a gas can sitting on the floor.

"We flush them out with that."

"Are you going to spit fire to ignite it?"

"Funny, but no. There are waterproof matches with that camping gear over there in the corner." Shelley pointed at a rolled up tent, four walking sticks, some outdoor chairs, and a red emergency bag full of supplies.

"Okay, but how do you plan to get to the house?"

"Like you said, when the security system goes down, they'll be distracted and panicked, right? We do it then."

"But what if someone puts a bullet in your head on the way there?"

"Think about it, Patty. You're supposed to be the smart one, aren't you? If there were more people out here, we'd be dead already, or the FBI would be dropping in with helicopters, whatever. Nobody's coming. My guess is, it's Sara, her kids, that wrinkled old babysitter, and then the two men you saw running inside."

"And both of them are wounded." She had to admit, Shelley had a point.

The fact that they weren't dead yet meant they still had a chance.

TWENTY

Sara stood over Teddy and tried to keep an eye out the back window, carefully watching the tool shed, wondering how Patty and Shelley had gotten inside. Teddy had been right. For all the money she'd spent on protecting her home, her family, someone with enough motive and resources had easily been able to get inside.

After a heated exchange between the group, and at Randall's insistence and Mary's confirmation, they'd chosen not to call the police. They had a better chance of ending this thing once and for all without the added intrusion of local law enforcement. Too many rules, too many restrictions, and yet another avenue for Patty and Shelley to live another day.

Sara had agreed to it, but wondered if they'd made the right decision.

Teddy was lying on her kitchen table, bleeding from the wound in his shoulder. As he'd thought, the bullet only grazed him. Irina poured hydrogen peroxide on it and cleaned the area around the bloody mess. In the living room, Randall hadn't been quite as lucky. Mary helped with his wound. Thankfully, the bullet had passed through his thigh, but the damage would need medical attention.

When that would happen was anyone's guess.

What a mess her life had become in the span of one single day. Again. Sara fought the tears that threatened to blur her vision yet again. When would it ever stop?

Tonight. It had to be tonight.

She wanted to be with her kids. Miss Willow had them in the panic room. Shut, locked and secure. Nothing short of a nuclear bomb would be able to harm them, and Sara felt safe in knowing that if anything happened to her or the rest of the group, then her children and Miss Willow could last for days in there; plenty long enough for help to arrive.

"Does it hurt?" Sara asked Teddy.

"Yes and…ouch! Honey, don't be so rough." Irina apologized and continued dabbing with the wet rag.

"How'd they get in, Teddy?"

"Some crazy device that blocked the lasers. We found it on the way back and my God, Sara, at first we thought they were already here because two of Randall's friends are dead back there in the woods."

"What?"

"Yeah, he'd called them in to help with surveillance, but it looks like Patty and Shelley got to them before they could warn us."

"Oh no, those poor guys." Sara's lip trembled. Two more people dead because of her. Two more people dead that had been trying to help a stranger. How high would the body count go?

"It was awful," Teddy said. He winced again as Irina applied a bandage. "We started sprinting as fast as we could because we thought for sure we'd get here and you guys would be dead. I've never been so damn scared, Sara. I thought we'd lost everyone and it was our fault for being idiotic enough to leave you guys alone." He managed to lift his wounded arm, put it around Irina, and pulled her close, kissing her hard on the lips. "Thank God you're okay."

"For now," Irina said, finishing up the bandage. She helped Teddy sit up.

In the living room, Randall cursed and said, "Easy, dammit. That ain't a piece of ham back there. And y'all in there in the kitchen, keep an eye on the shed, but don't stand right in front of the windows."

Irina kept watch while Sara and Teddy followed the sound of more curses and Randall's hissing as Mary tried to stop the blood flow. She wrapped a thick layer of gauze around his leg. If they weren't in danger, the sight might've been amusing—Randall, former Marine sniper and hardened country boy, lying on his stomach with his pants around his ankles. Tighty-whities on full display.

"T-bird," he said. "Looks like you got the better end of the deal."

"Sorry about that. Thanks for saving my life."

"Shit, son, it wasn't me. As fast as those little legs of yours were moving, you probably outran the rest of the bullets. Ow, dammit. Easy, Mary."

"Don't be such a pansy," Mary said. She finished tying the tourniquet around his thigh. "All done."

Randall hobbled to his feet as he pulled his pants back up. "New plan," he said. "No sense in trying to lead them away from here with the cars. If we set one single foot outside these doors, we'll get a toe shot off, or worse yet, something else."

"You can't run anyway," Mary reminded him.

"Right. So, seems to me, the best plan is for you guys to head down to the panic room with the young'ns and wait it out until the reinforcements arrive. You said your cop buddy and the feds had people on the way, right?"

Sara nodded. "He said so, but where are they?"

"With the kind of equipment these two have, it's a good possibility they got in undetected, so surely, if they didn't trigger your Fort Knox security system, some dude sitting behind a desk up in FBI headquarters, watching a monitored satellite feed didn't pick up on it either."

"Right. So if we all hide in the panic room and wait it out—"

"Not me. *You*."

Sara shook her head. "No way. You're not fighting this battle for me. I mean, my God, Randall, you barely know us. You too, Mary. There's plenty enough room in there for everyone to hide."

Randall shook his head. "Remember what we said earlier? You let the government get their hands on this woman, she'll walk in three to five and you'll be right back in this situation. No doubt about it. We gotta fight back, Sara. Again, that's why we said no cops. My trigger finger is getting twitchy, my damn leg hurts, and I'm gonna shoot to kill."

"Then I'm doing it with you, and you're not changing my mind. My house, my kids, my rules."

"Me too," Teddy said. "They shot me."

"I'm staying," Irina added from her spot in the kitchen. "They shot my husband. My family…we don't run from that."

Sara watched Randall waffle over this in his mind. He grunted. "Fine, but you all need to stay out of the way. Don't make yourself an easy target and don't even think about opening a door. T-bird, what I'll need you to do is stay with me. You know your way around a gun, so you'll be down here and we'll catch them on the way in. They didn't come all this way to hang out in a damn shed and then retreat. Okay by you?"

"Roger that, boss."

Randall continued, "Mary, you keep an eye on Sara and do recon from upstairs. These two ladies will get impatient soon enough and after that," he said, snapping his fingers, "shoot to kill. One and done."

Sara took a deep breath and felt her lungs tighten with anticipation. Was this really it? The final showdown? She wanted to believe Barker, that the FBI would swoop in and save them from Patty Kellog and Shelley Sergeant, and that they would never have to worry about it again, but what Randall had said made sense. Behind closed doors, where deals were made, Patty was worth more alive than dead, regardless of whether or not she'd been trying to murder an innocent family.

Even if she tried to call Barker to let him know, would her call get through while he was on the flight?

She didn't have time to consider it. They had to move forward *now*. Randall was right. There would be no mercy for her enemies.

"Sounds like a plan," she said, "but I'm not hiding. I can shoot."

"Sara...there ain't no way I'm letting you—" He stopped mid-sentence as the lights went out. A beat later, a generator rumbled to life outside and the red glow of emergency lighting illuminated the house. "They cut the power?"

"Not from outside, no. There were too many redundancies built in."

"Then how?"

Teddy said, "The bigger question is, we've got lights, but the security system is backed up to the generator, right?"

"It's supposed to be," Sara said. "But...oh Jesus."

"What?"

"As far as I know, the systems had to be shut down internally."

Randall asked, "Meaning what?"

"The security company. She must have somebody on the inside." Sara put her hand to her forehead. "Irina, can you do me favor?"

"Of course."

"Run downstairs and check the monitors that I showed you earlier. Plus, there's a control board off to the right. Let us know if everything seems like it's on."

"Got it." Irina dashed over to the doorway leading down to the basement and disappeared around the corner.

Teddy asked, "You think Patty paid someone off?" He took Irina's place, surveying the back yard from a kitchen window.

Sara nodded.

"And we're sitting ducks?"

"Maybe."

Mary removed her pistol from its holster, grabbed Sara's arm, and pulled. "Come with me."

"What're we doing?"

"Upstairs. We need distance between you and them. You guys okay down here?"

Randall saluted Mary and Teddy copied him. Randall hobbled into the kitchen with Teddy on his heels.

From down in the basement, Irina called up. "Sara?"

"Everything okay?"

"All the monitors are out. No lights on the control board either."

Sara covered her mouth as Mary tugged on her arm. "Oh God."

Irina said, "Do you want me to come up or should I help Miss Willow with the kids?"

"Oh God, oh God, uh...please go stay with them. Do not open that door for anything, not until you hear me again, and me only. You know the code, right?"

"Yes," Irina called back, her voice trailing off as she raced to the far end of the basement.

"Will it work with the power off?" Mary asked. "Can she get in?"

"Yeah, the panic room has its own power and operates totally independent of the rest of the house. I made sure that they made it possible because I didn't want anyone being able to short the system and take control of it."

"Perfect, but we need to move, now."

Sara paused, resisting against Mary's coaxing grip. She couldn't decide whether it was more important to be with her children at the moment, locked inside the panic room where it was safe, or outside with the rest of them, fighting her own battles. If anything happened to her—and she prayed that it wouldn't—then Miss Willow would be their legal guardian. Beyond that, Teddy and Irina had offered their care.

"Should I go be with them?" she asked Mary.

"Your call. We can handle it, definitely."

"But if something happens to one of you..." Total strangers, risking their lives for her, while her children were locked inside a steel box which was a foot thick, capable of withstanding Armageddon.

Go, stay. Go, stay. Go, fight.

A deep rage welled inside her. She'd been angry

before, upset and scared, but this was pure wrath—
flaming snakes slithering around inside her chest.

*No more. This is it. I'm sick of this shit. They've made our
lives hell for too long, and I want to watch them burn.*

She said to Mary, "Give me a gun."

"No, Sara, it's better that—"

"Gun, Mary."

Mary nodded. She pulled a snub-nosed .38 from
her ankle holster and gave it to Sara. "You know how
to use that?"

"Point and pull the trigger. How hard can it be?"

"Up you go."

Sara took the steps in twos while Mary followed,
unable to climb as fast, damaged leg holding her back.
Step, push with the cane, and then do it again.

Up on the second floor, Sara threw open Jacob's
bedroom door. His window had the best view of the
rear of the property, especially the tool shed in the
distance. She put her back against the wall and eased
her head around to survey the back yard.

Mary joined her on the opposite side. "See
anything?"

"Nothing yet. I didn't realize that row of pine trees
was in the way. I can only see half the building."

Downstairs, she heard Randall and Teddy opening
two of the windows, followed by silence. They waited,

listening intently, watching for Patty or Shelley to rush for the house. Sara's breathing was heavy, partly in anticipation, partly from bitter seething.

If she got the chance, she hoped she would be the one to end it. But, maybe it was better to let Randall or Mary take care of it—maybe even Teddy—as long as she got to watch. How dare these two evil beasts try to ruin her life, her children's lives, all because they held grudges for things Sara hadn't done.

She hadn't *made* Brian want to leave Shelley.

She hadn't been the one to force Patty into the mental institution. She'd been there, she'd been a witness, but she was innocent. She'd spent a lot of time in therapy to convince herself of that after Patty's last assault.

Stupid, petty, resentful motherfuckers. Come into my house. Do it. I dare you.

Downstairs, Randall raised his voice in warning. "We've got movement. One bogey moving from the northeast. No clear line, Mary. You got a shot?"

Mary took a firing position and examined the area. "No shot. Pine trees in the way."

"Find a north-facing window," he shouted. "I'm sending Teddy that way down here. Whichever one it is, looks like she's carrying a gas can."

"Not good," Mary said. "Sara, you go across the

hall. Use that window, and let me know if you see her."

"Okay." Sara darted out the door in front of Mary, swinging around the top of the stairs with one hand on a banister. She flew into her master bedroom, slung back the curtains, and opened the window. One quick peek outside—she saw nothing—and then she pulled her head back in.

Sara held steady, tried to control her breathing, and looked again.

Nothing.

Two shots boomed below, trailed by Teddy's voice. "I missed! I missed! Northwest corner, Sara, hurry!"

One, two, three shots from Mary in the north-facing bathroom. "Shit!"

Sara leaned out the window and down below her, thirty feet away, stood Shelley Sergeant holding a can of gas with her back against the western side of the house.

"Got you." Sara aimed and felt the trigger moving underneath her finger.

TWENTY-ONE

Sara squeezed the trigger harder and felt it give. The shot boomed and made her ears ring. Down below, Shelley screamed as the bullet ripped a hole in the siding, missing her head by inches. Sara fired again, and a crater opened in a cinderblock near Shelley's feet. Sara cursed and steadied her aim with both hands.

Shelley covered her head with one arm and scrambled for safety, pouring the gas along the ground as she went.

Sara fired a third time and missed yet again.

Three more steps and Shelley flung herself forward, diving underneath the front porch.

Sara screamed, "Randall!"

"You get her?"

"No, she made it under the front porch, still has the gas can with her."

"We're on it. Teddy? Come watch the back yard."

Sara listened to them changing positions downstairs; Randall's boots thumping across the hardwood floors. His steps were erratic, evidence of his wounded leg. She ran out of her bedroom, down the hall, and into the northernmost bathroom, hoping for a better angle. She could see down the edge of the porch, but there was no sign of Shelley.

Outside, in the hallway, Mary thumped along with her bum leg and cane, heading back to the first room with the view of the shed.

Sara called after her. "Mary? What do we do?"

"Stay there. Let Randall try to flush her out from downstairs. If she makes a break for it from your side, don't be shy about pulling that trigger."

"No chance of that."

"Don't forget to lead her a little. Shoot where she's going to be—whoa, movement! Movement back at the shed! Teddy, where are you?"

His calm voice traveled up the stairs. "I see her."

Pop, pop, pop.

"Missed! Damn it, she's fast!"

"Where's she going?"

"Moving toward the south side of the house."

"Sara," Mary said, "what's around there? Anything she can use for cover?"

Sara tried to remember but her mind went blank. Jesus, why couldn't she remember what was on the south side of her own house?

Empty, her mind was empty, and she couldn't recall a picture of what was—yes! "Nothing but a dogwood tree, but she can get under the front porch from that side, too."

ERNIE LINDSEY

"Get there, Teddy," Mary said.

"On it."

"Randall? ...Randall?"

Sara could sense the growing panic in Mary's voice. She stuck her head out the window, craning her neck to see underneath the porch. The front screen door slammed and beneath the awning, she saw Randall's lower half, moving cautiously. She tried to whisper loudly across the hall. "I see him. He's okay."

At the south side of the house, Sara heard the sound of breaking glass, followed by the *pop, pop* of Teddy's handgun. He screamed, "Got her! Wait, no. Son of a bitch. She's moving."

Across the hallway, Mary shouted, "Sara, tell Randall to back out. Back out now!"

Sara didn't hesitate. She screamed, "Get in the house, Randall."

Shots were fired from a distance, too far away to be Randall. Underneath the awning, she watched him pitch to the side, spin, and fall. He climbed up to his hands and knees, jumped, propelling himself through the open doorway just as orange flames began to lick up from underneath the porch. She stood, mesmerized, watching how quickly the wood became engulfed, travelling down the side of the house. The fact that it had rained didn't seem to make a difference.

The siding took to the flame like dry kindling in a fireplace.

Sara screamed, "Fire!" and ran for the door. She hit the top of the stairs as Mary came out of the bedroom. "Front of the house is going up."

"It's already around the back, too."

"What do we do?" she asked, descending the stairs.

"As far as we know, they're trapped under the front porch. We get to a spot where we can monitor both open ends and catch them when they come out. Porch is on fire, they'll have nowhere to go."

Sara shook her head. "Not true."

"What?"

"There's a small entrance under the porch that leads to the crawl space. It's like, maybe twenty square feet where a lot of the piping is, but they can get into the basement from there."

At the bottom of the steps, they found Teddy and Randall together in the living room, watching out the front picture window.

Sara said, "Randall, are you hurt? Did she get you?"

"I'm good, but I was about a half inch away from catching lead with my teeth. Did I hear you say they can get into the basement from under the front porch?"

"Yeah."

"So that means they're already in the house."

"Would they climb *into* a burning house?" Teddy asked.

Mary said to him, "They know we've got them covered from outside. They get into the basement, there's more room to hide."

Randall asked, "And they for sure can't get into the panic room, right?"

"Not a chance."

"And it's fireproof all around? Like if this house went up in flames, it wouldn't melt the wiring or get into the ventilation system in there, anything like that?"

"No. They're safe."

"Good." He moved toward the door leading down to the basement.

"Where are you going?" Mary asked.

"To shoot some people."

"Hang on a sec," Teddy said. "If they're inside the house, and it's burning, and then everyone is safe in the panic room, why don't we go outside and wait on them? Unless they want to die in here, they'll try to get out, won't they?"

Randall grinned. "I'll be damned, T-bird, that

actually makes some sense." He put a hand on Sara's shoulder. "You got anything in this house you wanna rescue before we roast some marshmallows on it?"

There wasn't much time to think. Outside, the flames had crawled up the siding and had reached the windows. In a few seconds, their escape routes would be cut off. After Patty had blown up Sara's last home in Portland, all of their personal things that held memories had evaporated. Since they'd been here in southwest Virginia, they hadn't had much time to build a life or to create memories. They had new furniture, new rooms, new clothes, but no roots.

Sara shook her head. "Let it burn."

***

They went out the rear entrance. Randall led the way, followed by Mary, Teddy, then Sara. The flames were lighter in back because Shelley had only managed to get a small amount of gas on that side of the house. Randall looked left and right, checked again, and led them out. "Clear," he said.

Sara was too far away, but she swore she could feel the heat on her cheeks.

Maybe it was fear instead of fire.

Teddy said, "How do we know they're in the basement already?"

"We don't," Randall answered. "Somebody's gotta go check. Let's put a little distance between us first. Mary, you take the north side. Teddy, south, and then Sara, you get over there to that little outbuilding. What's in there?"

"Lawnmower," she answered.

"All right, get in there, and I only want you to stick your nose out if you got a shot, okay? And don't get your nose shot off in the process."

"Where are you going?"

"To check under the front porch."

"Be careful," Mary said. "Be a hero all you want, but you're going home tonight."

"Yes, ma'am. No doubt about it."

Sara watched them hug—their bond was unmistakable after what they'd been through the previous year. She'd gotten some of the details from Mary while Randall and Teddy were gone, and the pure insanity of that situation would've hardened anyone. When all of this was over, she'd be sure to sit down with Randall and exchange stories about the deadly games they'd both played.

She stood and watched the flames dance up the side of the house and a strange feeling came over her.

How absurdly odd was it knowing that her children—and Miss Willow, and Irina—were inside a house that was about to become a smoldering pile of charred ash, yet they were completely safe?

Regardless of the hundreds of thousands of dollars she'd spent on a security system that Patty and Shelley had infiltrated easily, the panic room was the smartest decision she'd made concerning their safety.

She hated to watch the house go. She'd grown to love it and the property over the past few months, but maybe it was a blessing. A moment of finality, signifying the end to her fears, her past, and these godforsaken games.

Let it burn, she'd said.

Damn right.

She felt Teddy's arms around her. He said, "You be safe," and kissed the side of her forehead. She returned the embrace and told him to do the same. "And," she added, "so help me God, if you let anything happen to yourself and I have to face Irina's wrath, I will hunt you down in the afterlife and kick your scrawny little ass."

"If that happens, Irina will beat you to it."

"Time's wasting," Randall said. "Everybody ready?"

Three heads nodded in unison.

"Shoot to kill," he said. "If the feds don't know yet that these two are here, who knows when the cavalry will show up. We can't let them get their hands on Patty."

Teddy jogged south, using the row of pine trees as concealment. Mary hobbled north, pushing herself with her cane around the flowerbeds, staying low behind the snowball bushes and the cherub water fountain. Randall, who must have been high on adrenaline, moved faster than a man with a bullet hole in his leg should've been able to. He went straight for the house, cut north, holding his pistol down by his waist, and then vanished around the side. The last Sara saw of him was the vestige of his body behind the orange flames.

She took one last look at the house, sighed, and then jogged over to the outbuilding.

Inside, it smelled like oil and wet rags. She crouched and left the door open just enough to get a view of the house. She couldn't see Mary from her position, but to the south, Teddy squatted behind a lilac bush. She watched him peek through the branches, carefully observing, with his 9mm Glock up and ready.

She put a knee down on the ground to balance herself. The dirt floor felt cool through her jeans. She'd been meaning to have concrete poured, but hadn't gotten around to it. Now, as the flames engulfed her home, it seemed like such an innocuous thing to fret about. She hadn't heard any shots from Randall yet, so they had to have retreated to the basement.

How much longer would Shelley and Patty last inside? What were they doing?

Were they now doubting their decision? It hadn't been the wisest approach. Surely they'd had other plans. Perhaps another game for her and her children, but had the presence of Randall and Teddy thrown them off course?

Thank God she'd approached Randall, and then Randall had called Mary in—if it hadn't been for the two of them, everyone—she and the kids, Miss Willow, Teddy and Irina—would likely be dead.

Small miracles. Timing. Good people.

Those things saved lives.

A porch column collapsed and the overhang slumped to one side. The entirety of the exterior was nearly covered in flames and had begun to spread inside. Soon, the heat would be unbearable.

How long before one of the neighbors noticed and called the fire department. Sara knew there were no full time firemen on staff—they were all volunteers who lived in the surrounding area. What was their average response time if they had to get the call, get from their homes to the fire station, and then all the way out here on the outskirts of town? Fifteen minutes at the least, right?

Could Patty and Shelley last that long inside? Could they wait it out?

What would happen if the fire department arrived and two armed and highly dangerous murderers were still alive in her basement? What then?

Would they surrender? Would they shoot their way out?

Patty probably knew that the government would keep her alive for information. She would surrender and live to fight another day. But Shelley, that crazy girl had a death wish. Hadn't her brother Michael told her that back in the cabin, during the game, ages ago? That Shelley wasn't afraid of death? Or had that been a part of the dreams that haunted her since?

A window shattered from the heat on the second floor. Sara watched the flames overtake Jacob's curtains.

As the fire lit up the night sky, she held her breath and waited, wanting nothing more than the chance to shoot first.

TWENTY-TWO

Patty shoved Shelley as hard as she could, watching as the one-eyed girl sailed backward and fell into the pool table. Shelley hit with enough force that her legs lifted off the ground, sending her on top of it, scattering pool cues and balls across the green felt. "Any more genius ideas?"

Shelley groaned and rolled off the pool table, holding her lower back.

Patty marched over, grabbed her by the hair, and yanked her hard to the side. "Come here. Come look at this." She dragged a dazed Shelly over to a large metal door and then pounded on it with her fist. "You see that? Panic room. I don't know who's in there and my guess is it's her little parasites, but you know what? It doesn't matter, because we're not getting in there, and instead, we're trapped in the goddamn basement of a burning fucking house, you idiot."

Shelley tried to pull free, reaching for Patty's face.

Patty thrust her head to the side, held on, and dragged Shelley to the side and slammed her against the wall. "I don't know why I thought I might care about someone so stupid. I trusted you. I thought you were better than this, and now you've gotten us trapped down here. I don't even know how many people were up there, and they sure as hell aren't any more. Three? Four, five, ten? How many, Shelley? If you'd listened to me, we could've walked away. We could be meeting my guy and we could be on our way out of the country, but no, I let you talk me into this reckless—God, what was I thinking, huh?" Patty clenched her jaws so tightly, her head hurt. "And then...I couldn't let you go. I had to come make sure you weren't dead. So that's my fault. Right? That's on me. What do we do now, huh? Tell me, Shelley, what's next? Do we die down here in the fire, or do we die trying to shoot our way out?"

"Let me go," Shelley whimpered, "and I'll show you something."

"It better be good." Patty released Shelley's hair, but finished with a hand to her face, and a hard shove against the wall before backing away. "Show me what?"

Shelley moved over to the control panel on the exterior of the panic room. A standard keypad, numbered zero through nine, along with alphabetized letters sat in a receding hole in the wall. "People are creatures of habit, right?"

"I suppose."

"How many different passwords do you use for all of your accounts?"

"The house is burning down, we don't have time for twenty questions."

"Seriously, how many?"

Patty shook her head and put her hands on her hips. "Three, at the most. Same password for email addresses or bank accounts, same PIN for ATMs or anything like…" The realization hit her. "No, you don't think she would…"

Shelley winked with her remaining eye. "I worked for her. I was her secretary, her lackey, her errand girl and her whipping post for so long. Do this for me, do that for me, pick up my kids, pick up my dry cleaning, can you get twenty bucks in cash out for me…same old shit, all the time, and *in* that time, you want to know how many different passwords and PINs she used? Two. Two, and that's it. The idiot kept her stupid email password written on a yellow sticky note beside her computer at work. Yeah, she was some kind of marketing genius, but she couldn't remember her own phone number or what color shirt—"

"The house is burning, the house is burning, the house is burning! Stop being The History Channel and open it up."

Shelley held a hand above the keypad and paused,

her finger hovering over the first number. "What if it doesn't work?"

"Then I shoot you in the head and take my chances."

"Fair enough." She punched in the sequence, reciting the numbers as she went. "One, eight, four, eight. Her dead husband was dumb enough to use the same one, too. Here goes…" Shelley pressed the green button on the lower right side of the panel.

A set of red LED lights blinked three times in rapid succession, then went green, one by one. The door slid to the side, revealing three frightened children, Miss Willow the babysitter, and a woman that Patty had never seen before. No Sara, and neither of the two wounded men.

Miss Willow and the children recoiled when they saw Shelley standing in the doorway with a demented smile.

"Hi, guys," Shelley said as she waved. "Remember me?"

Patty had a feeling that those four words were the most frightening ones the children had ever heard. When they began to scream, she knew she was right. Patty had to laugh. She said to Shelley, "I thought panic rooms were supposed to *cure* panic, huh?"

"I know, right?"

Sara's kids squeezed as close to Miss Willow as they possibly could, wailing those annoying sirens of fear. Mouths wrenched down and to the side in terror, clinging to the old woman's sweater.

Miss Willow said, "I knew the Devil would come back one of these days."

Shelley chuckled. "Speak of her and she shall appear."

The blonde woman said, "Get away from us."

"Who're you?"

"Teddy's wife. My name is Irina."

"Sucks to be you," Patty said. "Out. All of you. Out, now!" She waved her gun, and when none of them moved, she lifted it and fired two shots into the ceiling. The children screamed and covered their ears. Miss Willow scrambled to her feet, pulling the twins with her, while the woman named Irina helped the little boy get up.

Miss Willow asked, "Is that smoke? Is the house on fire?"

Shelley laughed. "It is, and we need to get out of here now. Even the Devil gets warm in Hell."

"You...you...evil—"

Shelley grabbed the old woman's arm, pulled her close, and put the barrel of her handgun against Miss Willow's forehead. "You can die right here, or you can help us get the children outside, then you die. Choose."

"Okay, okay. I'll help, just don't hurt them. Please."

"That's what I thought."

Patty said to Irina, "You, up the stairs. Go see if the fire's blocking any of the doors."

"No."

Patty pointed her gun, pulled the trigger, and shot a hole in the floor near Irina's feet. Irina screamed and jumped backward. Patty said, "Go find us a way out, or you die right here. *We* don't need you, but they do." Patty pointed at Sara's children. "Go. And believe me, if you run, or try to come back down here with some kind of weapon, anything stupid like that, I will not think twice about pulling the trigger on one of these little beauties."

"I understand." Irina kissed Lacey, Callie, and Jacob on the head. "I'll be right back. We're gonna go find Mommy, okay?" All three nodded. Irina dashed across the basement and up to the ground floor.

Smoke drifted in from crevices and air ducts.

Patty said to Shelley, "Over to the stairs. We need to be ready."

Shelley put a hand on Miss Willow's back and shoved, then grabbed Jacob's arm and dragged him with her. Patty followed with the twins.

They congregated at the bottom of the steps as Miss Willow tried to comfort the coughing children. Above, Patty listened to the panicked footsteps as Irina ran back and forth. Maddening seconds ticked by as they waited. She'd sent Irina to go look, assuming that she would need Shelley downstairs to help her keep an eye on Miss Willow and the children, and now, that didn't seem to be the wisest option. Would Irina be selfish enough to escape and leave them behind? Would she be stupid enough to hunt for a weapon while she was up there?

I should've sent Shelley. God, what was I thinking?

Patty said, "She's got ten seconds, Shelley, then you're going after her."

"Okay."

Patty counted to herself. Something crashed against the floor overhead. Was it furniture collapsing? Were the walls caving in already?

She could feel the smoke seeping into her lungs. It burned when she breathed and tasted like ashes on her tongue. She watched as Miss Willow helped the children hold their shirts over their noses and mouths. Up the stairs and out one of the doors would be easier, but should they risk trying to escape the way she and Shelley had entered, through the crawlspace?

"Shelley," she said, "get up there."

261

And before her partner could move, the blonde woman appeared at the top of the stairs. "Back door, let's go!"

"Is it clear?"

"Barely." She glanced to her side and frantically waved them up. "Hurry!"

Patty and Shelley grabbed, dragged, and pulled Miss Willow and the children along, their footsteps pounding up and up to where the smoke hung thick and the orange flames enveloped the walls, the furniture, and the curtains. The heat was intense, unlike anything she'd ever felt before. When they all emerged into the living room, Patty shoved Irina and Miss Willow, and held her gun to their faces. "Lead us out."

They paused, exchanging knowing looks. They were one doorway from their deaths.

"Move," Patty said. "Die here or help us get them outside."

Irina and Miss Willow moved toward the rear of the house, hunched over beneath the layer of smoke. They stayed toward the center of the living room, avoiding the fire, and then scampered across the hallway, through the kitchen, and up to the back door.

Shelley yelped and swung her arm. She'd brushed against something and her sleeve was on fire. She slapped at it until the flames disappeared.

Irina touch the doorknob and hissed. "It's too hot," she said.

"Do something," Patty ordered.

Irina turned her shoulder and forced herself against the door. It flew outward and banged against the outside wall, sending a shower of embers floating through the air. Half of the porch's overhang had collapsed, but they had enough room to escape in the space that remained. The children coughed, cried, and followed when Miss Willow coaxed them, urging them to hurry.

Shelley grabbed Lacey, and Patty grabbed Callie, using them as human shields.

"What now?" Shelley asked.

"Once we get outside, drop those two," she said, pointing to the backs of Irina and Miss Willow, "and then make sure anyone out there knows we've got her kids. Sara, definitely."

"Got it."

They walked briskly underneath the burning overhang and out into the night, where the air was fresh, clean, and moist.

Patty lifted her weapon. Shelley lifted hers.

They each fired a single shot.

Irina dropped first. Miss Willow stumbled, took another step, and went down.

The children screamed and covered their eyes.

Patty shouted, "Sara! Tell your friends to back off, wherever they are. You shoot, they shoot, anyone shoots, your children die." She waited for a response. "Do you hear me? Where are you?"

"Here! I'm here! Don't hurt them."

Patty scanned the back yard, looking for the origin of Sara's voice. The dancing flames at her back brightened the night, giving her a mottled glimpse of Sara as she stepped out of the small building, holding her hands over her head.

"Tell your people, Sara! Tell them."

"They can hear you."

To her right, Patty heard a familiar male voice screaming, "Irina!" and when she glanced around, Teddy Rutherford sprinted toward his motionless wife. It had been a while since she'd seen such anguish, and for a single second, she paused to enjoy it. Relishing in the pain of others had always been one of her favorite things.

"I got him," Shelley said, whipping her arm to the right. She pulled the trigger.

Pop.

Teddy pitched hard to the side and went down.

So easy.

TWENTY-THREE

When Sara first heard the muffled shots, she assumed she had allowed her worst fears to take over her mind. They couldn't be shots, could they? No, it had to be the sound of popping timbers as the fire consumed the farmhouse. Or, maybe if Shelley and Patty were the only two inside, they were after each other, locked in a duel and turning on each other.

Sara felt her spirits rise a little. She held her breath in anticipation. Should she feel hope instead of agonizing desperation?

Another muffled pop and this time, it was unmistakable.

That was definitely a gunshot. What's going on in there?

Was that the final bullet to end one of their lives?

She imagined Patty standing over Shelley, pointing the gun at the younger woman's chest, and then firing. Better yet, perhaps one was dead and the other was badly wounded, and rather than perishing in the fire, she chose to end it all. That would be the preferable option. Both dead and gone; she and the children and Miss Willow could move on with their lives.

Finally, after all this time.

She took a moment to consider the aftermath—

would they rebuild here on the farmland, or was this another infected place? Two evil souls would escape burning flesh in the basement of her home, damning the land underneath it. Contaminating the soil, destined to haunt the place for eternity where their horrible lives had ended. All that bad energy released into the world...maybe it was better that her family was far away from it.

They would sell the land and move yet again. Maybe to a tropical island. Hawaii was nice. She had the money. They could go and bring her parents with them, who had been discussing spending the remainder of their retirement in a sandy, ocean-side climate.

Even though she was watching her house burn, and her children, Miss Willow, and Irina were inside contained within that hulking steel container—they would be buried under the smoldering rubble but safe—she felt a sense of calm overcome her.

This was the end. They'd made it. Her worst fears had come true, and they had survived them.

And then, the house of optimism she'd built in her mind crumbled as Irina and Miss Willow emerged from the back door, followed by her children, and then those two wretched monsters, Patty Kellog and Shelley Sergeant.

She stifled a scream and froze in fear.

Oh my God, how did she get them out? How was it poss—the entry code. Shelley remembered. How could I be so stupid?

You thought she was in prison and three thousand miles away, that's how.

But Miss Willow had been begging you to change it for months. So stupid.

Two individual gunshots sent Irina and Miss Willow to the ground. Sara bit her lip hard enough to taste blood and an overpowering wave of nausea hit her stomach. Were they dead? She hadn't been able to tell where the shots went, but now they were lying on the ground, motionless. She'd gotten to know Irina better over the past few months, but Willow was a family member who had been a mother when Sara's own was three thousand miles away.

She stood, arm raised, pistol up and ready to come out firing when Patty screamed, "Sara! Tell your friends to back off, wherever they are. You shoot, they shoot, anyone shoots, your children die." She waited for a response. "Do you hear me? Where are you?"

"Here! I'm here! Don't hurt them." Sara stepped out of the building, holding her arms over her head. Mary's .38 revolver remained tucked in the waistband at her back.

"Tell your people, Sara! Tell them."

"They can hear you."

To Patty's right, Teddy's gut-wrenching wail of "Irina!" made Sara pause. She watched as he sprinted at them, ignoring Patty and Shelley, focused only on the love of his life, the woman who loved and endured him, as she lay on the ground, either dead or dying.

For a moment, everything slowed. Sara watched Teddy as he pumped his arms and legs, propelling himself across the yard. She looked at Patty, fearing the worst, and then it happened…Shelley's arm went up, fire erupted from the barrel, and Teddy stumbled and went down.

"Stop!" Sara screamed. She tried to move. Her legs had become hardened tree trunks and had grown roots. She was paralyzed, unable to move, as she watched Teddy writhing on the ground.

Shelley tried to shoot again, but Patty grabbed her arm, laughed, and said, "Let him suffer, Shell. It'll be fun watching him die trying to save this moron." She kicked Irina's limp leg. Irina's head moved, slightly, and it gave Sara an inkling of hope.

But Miss Willow…nothing.

Lacey, Callie, and Jacob stood where they were, looking so afraid that they weren't able to scream. Sara thought about telling them to run but she was afraid of what Patty's reaction might be. Shelley's too.

Shelley had locked them in boxes before and would've murdered them, given the chance. Patty could've easily blown them up with two different bombs if it hadn't been for Vadim Bariskov's warning.

Sara remained silent. If she screamed for them to run, if they managed to break free, they would be shot.

"Where are the rest of your people, Sara?"

"I don't know."

"Where are they? Get them out here where I can see them or...or...which one is this?"

"Lacey."

Patty yanked a handful of hair.

"Mommy!"

"It's okay, honey."

"Sara, get them out here or she's the first to go. Where are the rest? I saw them. *Where* are they?"

Sara yelled for Mary, then said to Patty, "She's the only one that made it out. And Teddy, too."

"Bullshit. Don't lie to me, Sara. Where's the tall one?"

Sara lied. "After—after we heard you shooting, he went back inside, trying to figure out what was happening."

"Do you want to see her brains all over the ground? Do *not* lie to me. Where is he?"

"I don't know."

"He has ten seconds. And Mary? Did you say Mary?"

Damn it, where are you, Randall? Why aren't you here? We need you. Please, God, help us.

Sara walked across the yard, slowly, step by agonizing step. They watched her with smiles on their faces as she paused within twenty feet. Behind them, the house was completely engulfed in flames that danced inside and licked around the doors, windows, and awnings.

To her right, Mary hobbled out of the shadows, limping and leaning on her cane, holding her pistol by the trigger guard. It dangled over her head from her index finger. Neither Shelley nor Patty had noticed her yet, and when they did, they whipped their weapons around, telling her to drop it and stay where she was.

"I'm sorry, Sara," Mary said.

"It's okay."

Shelley fired a single shot over Mary's head. "Get your friend out here."

"He went back inside. She's not lying."

Sara lied, "It's the truth, Patty."

Mary added, "He's an ex-Marine. Trust me, if he was still alive, you'd be dead already. I know you don't believe me, but that's the truth."

Patty and Shelley exchanged glances. Patty said,

"You keep believing that."

Teddy tried to army crawl toward them, yelling "Irina," again and again.

Sara said, "Teddy, stay right there before they shoot you."

"No!"

"Please, stay."

He rolled onto his back and screamed at the sky.

In the distance, she heard the faint sound of sirens. Someone had reported the fire. But, the way the undulating noise carried through the nearby valleys, she couldn't be sure of how far away they were. Did it matter? Would they be able to get past the front security gate?

Wait, they'd disabled the system. Okay, okay, maybe the gate is open.

"What do you want?" she asked Patty and Shelley. "Haven't you done enough already? You murdered my husband, you've tried to murder my children. Our homes—you've destroyed our homes and chased me thousands of miles. If it's me—if it's *only* me, just pull the trigger and be done with it, but let them go. Let my babies go."

"What fun would that be, Sara?" Patty asked. "We've both been waiting for this for so long. We've suffered for *so* long while you got everything you wanted, didn't you? Life just keeps handing you all the good stuff while we're stuck down here in the shit—prison, murdering people for a living—it's not exactly the most exciting career path, you know. Look at you now, huh? How is it that you've escaped us twice, and things just keep getting better for you each time? Tell me how that's possible. Karma? Is it karma? You've dealt with enough shit that now the universe hands you millions upon millions of dollars while Shelley rots in her cell, afraid that one of those goons in prison will gouge out her other eye…is that it?"

"No, I don't know—please, let the kids go, you can have—"

"What? We can have the *money*, Sara? That's why you think we're doing this? This is payback. A reckoning. Yeah, maybe money can buy that for some people but what we want, what we've been waiting years for, is to watch you suffer. That's it. That's all."

"You can have that. Whatever you want. Let the kids go and I'll do whatever you want. Let them go and I'll walk into the house. I'll walk in there, I'll stand in the middle of the floor and I'll swallow fire if you want."

Shelley chuckled and said to Patty, "That's actually a pretty good idea."

"I thought so, too." Patty held the barrel of her

gun to Lacey's head. "Go," she ordered, flicking her chin toward the house.

"Not until they're free." Sara didn't know if it would matter. If she walked into the house and if she stood there and consumed fire like she'd offered, Patty and Shelley absolutely would not walk away. They would finish off Teddy. They would put a bullet between Mary's eyes, and then her children.

No consciences. No witnesses. Nothing but death and another bloodbath in the small, southwestern Virginia town. The second one in two years. Massive, multiple murders…and it would be their names in the newspapers.

"Fine." Patty pushed Lacey over to Shelley. "Keep them here. I want them to watch."

Lacey, Callie, and Jacob screamed for Sara when they made eye contact. Reaching, reaching for her. Twenty feet away, but miles distant.

"Go to Mary," Sara said. "She'll keep you safe." Their screams were heartbreaking. "Please, go to Mary, okay? Do it for Mommy." They tried to lunge for her but Shelley yanked their arms, pulling them hard, and they went, reluctantly walking over to Mary where she wrapped her arms around them. They buried their faces in her chest.

Patty said, "Make them watch or I'll put a bullet in

each one of them. Right in the back of the head. Make them watch and I'll let you go."

"Liar," Mary said.

"You don't have a choice. Shelley, go—"

Mary relented. "Okay, stop. Just stop. Kids? Listen to me. Turn around and tell your mama you love her. She's being very brave for all of you."

Lacey, Callie, and Jacob turned to face her with tears pouring down their cheeks.

Lacey spoke first. "Love you, Mommy."

Then Callie. "Please don't go. I love you. Please stay."

And finally, Jacob, "Don't go in there, Mommy, please."

"It'll be okay, buddy. Mommy loves all of you so much."

It was absolutely heartbreaking, but she still had a chance.

Where is Randall? Where in God's name is he?

Patty put her arm around Shelley. "So touching, isn't it?"

"Makes me want to vomit."

"Sara, in you go. Into the house. Look's like Hell is waiting for you."

Sara nodded.

He'll come, won't he? Where is he? Where could he be?

Did he really go back inside? Maybe he'd tried to crawl under the house, through the crawlspace. Would he do that? Were those shots I heard from him? Was he trying to get our attention? Oh God. No. Please no. Give me hope. Something.

"Move, Sara."

Shelley laughed and said, "Hey, if you've got any popcorn in there, throw it out here."

Sara took a step, then another. She glanced over at Teddy. He'd passed out on the ground. From pain? From loss of blood. What did it matter anymore? Or was he dead?

She stepped around the bodies of Miss Willow and Irina.

Miss Willow hadn't moved since Shelley pulled the trigger.

Irina lay on her stomach, alive, but breathing heavily. The wound at her upper shoulder had drenched her white shirt so that the top half was dark red and caked with drying blood.

With Randall nowhere in sight, she felt her last remnant of faith fade away.

Where had he gone? Had he ran away? Had he decided that he had his own family to worry about?

Would I have done the same? Would I have put my life at risk to save strangers if the kids were waiting for me at home? I don't know.

She sighed.

This was it. Patty and Shelley had won. After all these years of torture and distress, agonizing over Brian's disappearance and enduring so many sleepless nights and near-mental breakdowns, escaping from Shelley's cage, avoiding Patty's bombs, saving her family twice from these two deranged individuals, this was the end.

Game over. She'd lost.

"You win," she said to them.

Patty smirked. "It's easy when you make the rules. Get in inside. Go on, before the thing collapses."

Sara arced around, keeping space between them. Her skin grew hotter as she stepped closer and closer to the dancing flames. Her cheeks were flushed.

She stopped at the foot of the porch steps, wondering if she could really do it. If everyone was going to die anyway, would it matter if she tortured herself like this? If they were all going to die, wouldn't it make more sense to go out fighting and take a bullet instead of allowing herself to be burned alive?

It would, and she almost turned, but instead...

Maybe Mary can do something if they're distracted. One last possibility, right?

If she sacrificed herself, maybe, just maybe, Mary would be able to pull off a miracle. Certainly more unbelievable things had happened in the world.

Do it, Sara. Up the steps.

Behind her, Patty shouted, "Up, up, up! I'm gonna count to three—"

"I'm going!" Sara lifted a foot and put it down on the bottom step. The heat was nearly unbearable. She coughed from the smoke and lifted another foot, set it down.

Another step.

And then another.

Flames whooshed around the porch column beside her and she smelled burning hair. The roar of the fire, the groaning, crackling, and popping wood muffled the sound of her children crying and for that, she was thankful.

One final step and she was on the porch.

A slight gust of wind blew the flame at her face. It licked her skin and she winced in pain.

Patty was right: Hell awaited. Inside the back door, it hadn't completely overtaken the farmhouse, but it wouldn't be long. She could still see some of the furniture and the walls through the thick smoke. With any luck, she would die of smoke inhalation before the flames took her body.

"Burn!" Shelley screamed. "Burn, you bitch. Burn!"

Sara held up her arm to block a dancing tongue of fire to her right and then, directly in front of her and across the far side of the house, the front door burst inward, splintering in pieces. Flaming shards scattered throughout the living room. Embers danced.

Randall fell through the opening, landed and rolled, then sprang to his feet—shirt on fire, flames clinging to his jeans—he thundered toward her, arm outstretched, aiming at her head with his pistol. A white rag was tied across his nose and mouth.

"Sara! Down!" he roared.

Sara flailed backward and dropped.

Randall jumped over her, airborne, flying across the porch, pulling the trigger as he went.

Four deafening shots exploded above her head.

Boom, boom. Boom, boom.

He fell to the porch, landing at the head of the stairs, and rolled down.

Sara swung herself around.

She saw Patty on her back, red soaking through her shirt. Immobile.

Shelley writhed where she lay, clutching her throat. Gagging, choking.

Up above, the porch overhang gave a final groan and collapsed, giving Sara a split second to dive down the steps and land on top of Randall. He rolled with her, holding his shoulder and grimacing.

When they came to a stop on the ground, he said, "Think I broke my collarbone."

Sara didn't know whether to hug him or smack him. "What took you so long?"

"Sorry. I'd be late to my own funeral."

"Yeah, well, that possibility was too close." She climbed to her feet and darted over to her children. She flung herself down to her knees and pulled them in for a hug. Laughing, crying, and overcome with relief.

"We did it," she said. "We won."

TWENTY-FOUR

The ambulance lights flashed across the hillside. They had been in such close proximity so many times. Red, the color of warning. Red, the color of blood.

Red, the end of another traumatic nightmare.

Sara sat on the open tailgate of a volunteer fireman's pickup, a blanket around her shoulders, a bottle of water in her hands. Behind her, Lacey, Callie, and Jacob had given in to exhaustion. They slept huddled together in a borrowed sleeping bag.

Across the way, the last remaining flames coughed and sputtered, trying to survive against the surge of a fire hose. The farmhouse was nothing more than a pile of charred, blackened, and smoldering timbers. Wisps of smoke drifted into the night sky.

Randall leaned up against the tailgate, his arm in a sling, bandages covering various spots of seared skin. Mary, bless her, had ridden to the hospital with Teddy and Irina. Both were in serious condition, but they would survive. If it hadn't been for Patty's desire to watch Teddy suffer, and Shelley's poor aim with one eye, both of her friends would likely be dead as well.

Sara watched in stunned silence as the paramedics lifted the black body bag inside the rear of an awaiting ambulance. Inside was the shell of Sara's friend and confidante, her rock and her second mother; despite their efforts to revive her, Miss Willow had already passed before the emergency personnel arrived.

Randall put an arm around Sara's shoulder. "I'm damn sorry about that."

"I've buried too many people," was all she could manage. True mourning would come later. For now, she'd already shed her tears—what remained was a fatigued absence of feeling.

A group of four FBI agents stood to their right, pointing at the house and talking in hushed voices with the local police.

"Can you believe those guys?" Randall asked. "Showing up late to the party like that, but still trying to take all the credit. Jesus H."

"They didn't scold you too much, did they?"

"Scold? Hell, they all thanked me, if you wanna know the truth. You wouldn't get them to say it under oath, but not a single one of them was on board with Morrow's plan to take Patty alive, and they all agreed that there should've been an active presence in the house. They still can't believe that Patty and Shelley got past their surveillance, and you won't hear them admit to that in public either. They're glad she's gone, though. Top secret info or not, she was a damn danger to society. Good riddance, bad rubbish, all that bullshit."

"So what's next?"

"Eh, I'll have to go in and answer some more questions. Debriefing and whatnot. I told them there wasn't much left to tell, but you know how the government is. They gotta spend time to waste more money."

"Yeah." Sara took a deep breath. She couldn't wait to see Randall give Morrow a piece of his mind when the agent in charge arrived. That would be fun to watch. As far as she knew, Barker and Morrow would be landing at Tri-Cities soon, then there would be the hour-long trek up I-81. So, at best, she would get to see Barker by two o'clock that morning. As soon as the agents saw fit to release them, she would head over to the hospital to check on Teddy and Irina.

Randall asked, "I think I already know the answer to this, but are you sticking around these parts?"

"I...maybe. Not *here* here, not on this property, but now that it's done and over with, I like it here. The country is just the right pace, it's beautiful, and the people are amazing. Seriously, where else would your neighbor fight a war for you?"

"We all fight some kind of war, Sara. The difference is whether you use emotions or bullets.

Either way, it's good to have somebody down in the trenches with you."

"That's true, but you and Mary risked your lives for us. That was above and beyond. What if you'd died? What about your family?"

"All in a day's work, ma'am. Serve and protect."

"Somehow I don't think your wife would think that's an acceptable answer."

"She's used to it."

Sara took a sip of her water and pulled the blanket tighter around her shoulders. "You know, Randall, for so long, I've been running away from bad memories and such evil people. One step ahead was one more day alive and I got sick of living that way. I've wondered if God might have it out for me, or if I was Hitler in a former life and karma is just now catching up—the past two or three years have been unreal. Every time, right when we thought our lives had come out on the other side of Hell, we'd get forced right back into the fire. But for all of that, for all of the evil that we've had to endure, you and Mary showed up to help us out. That was something *good*—you guys were a *blessing*, Randall—and as crazy as it sounds, I'd gotten to the point where I thought I'd never see pure decency again. Thank you."

"Ain't no big deal."

"Stop trying to downplay this. It's a *huge* deal, and I won't ever forget it. You won't ever have to want for anything again, I can tell you that much. Money, favors…anything, you just ask."

"Sara—"

She held up a finger to shush him. "No arguments. Look, I know that sounds like I'm putting some sort of monetary value on your kindness, but it's not about the money, it's not about buying our thanks, nothing like that. Being able to give what I can when *you* need it, that's the only way I'll ever be able to repay something like this."

"I'll tell you what," Randall said, pushing himself away from the truck bed. "Let's start with you buying me a beer one of these days. We'll say a prayer for Miss Willow, and drink a cold one in honor of T-bird and Irina for being such badasses. It takes a lot to eat lead and walk away from it. So those are my terms. One beer. Deal?"

"That'll never make us even."

"Maybe not in your eyes, but let me tell you what my grandpa told me: 'Give as much as you can and only take what you need.' If *everybody* lived by those rules, maybe the world wouldn't be knee-deep in bullshit."

***

After they'd gotten a ride to the hospital to see Teddy and Irina, a kind nurse with gray hair and a purple uniform had allowed Sara's children to fall asleep in the room next to the wounded Rutherfords.

Irina's injuries had been worse than Teddy's and she too slept peacefully in the bed by the window. In the low light of the room, Sara could see how pale her skin was. Irina had lost a lot of blood, but according to their doctor, she'd walk out in a couple of days.

Sara sat beside Teddy's bed, holding his hand.

He said, "So Miss Willow didn't make it, huh?"

She could only shake her head in response.

"Damn shame. Such a damn shame."

"I know. It's going to be hard without her and God, I feel like I'm shredding apart on the inside, but...you know, at least the kids are safe. You're okay. Irina's okay. I'm trying to see a silver lining."

"Yeah, about that," Teddy said. "Can you tell me something?"

"Sure."

"How am I the one that's in the hospital again? Really? I mean, *really*, how? Three times now, somebody has tried to murder you and *I'm* the one with an I.V. and a hospital bill. I think I need a

Winthrop clause in my insurance agreements."

It felt wrong to laugh, *so wrong*, but she did. Miss Willow was gone. Randall was wounded. Teddy and Irina had nearly died. Her children, yet again, would have another dose of trauma layered on top of everything they'd experienced. Resilient though they may be, right now, the damage would likely surface in a few years.

Her husband was dead. Detective Jonathan Johnson had died trying to protect her.

She was the root of so much death and destruction. It seemed fair to say that if a person had touched her life in some way, life would touch back, hard.

But she laughed anyway. It felt good to release the culmination of everything she'd held inside, trying to keep herself from breaking.

Teddy shook his head, smiling. "It's not *that* funny."

"I know," she said, dabbing at the corners of her eyes. "I'm sorry. It's just that—I mean…it's over. It's finally over and I'm so relieved but I feel like a tornado, you know? I can look back at these last couple of years and see the path of destruction I've left behind. I don't know why I'm laughing…I think it's because I can't cry anymore."

Teddy shook his head. "Nah, *you're* not the tornado, Sara. *Fate* is the tornado. Did you ever see that movie *Twister*? You're like that cow that gets picked up and tossed around and then the rest of us are trying to grab the cow and get it down out of the air to save its life. And then *we* end up in the hospital while the cow lands on its feet a mile away in the middle of some hayfield."

"Somehow, that actually makes sense."

"Not that you're a cow, obviously."

"Thanks for clarifying."

Irina stirred softly in her bed. Teddy tried to lean up to check on her, but the pain sent him onto his back. "Speaking of cows," he said, "are you staying here in Virginia?"

"Randall asked me the same thing. I think so. Or, at least this will be a home base, but for the moment I'm pulling the kids out of school and we're going away for a long while. Somewhere on an island with blue water, and as far away from civilization as possible. What about you guys? Still going on your honeymoon?"

"God, I hope so. We'll need the time to recoup. But, I don't know how Irina will feel about showing off a bullet wound in her bikini."

"Tell her to wear it like a badge of honor."

"Maybe I'll have a t-shirt made that says, 'I visited Sara Winthrop and all I got was this lousy scar.'"

"Fair enough."

Teddy put his arm behind his head. "Barker here yet?"

"He sent me a text and said he'll be here in a while. I'm just waiting on the showdown between Randall and that agent that's with Barker. Should be fun watching the fireworks."

"If I thought it'd change anything, I'd sue the guy right out of his suit."

"You could, but I have a feeling you can save your money. Randall has enough connections up in D.C. to have that guy scrubbing toilets in Antarctica."

"Good. Tell him to pack extra toothbrushes so he can really get into the corners."

The nurse poked her head inside the door. "Mrs. Winthrop? Your little boy's awake. He's asking for you."

Sara nodded. "Okay, tell him I'll be right there." She stood up and stretched. "Well, T-bird, looks like we survived another round together, huh?"

"No worse for wear."

"You asked me what *I'm* doing next...I know you've got the big release of your sniper game coming up, but are you guys staying in Portland after your honeymoon?"

Teddy shrugged. "We've talked about moving to Russia."

"Russia? Are you serious? Isn't it all corrupt and dangerous there?"

"It's probably safer than being around you."

Sara squeezed his hand one last time and glanced out the window.

The sun would be up in a few hours. The dawn of a new day.

Freedom under blue sky.

Author's Note

Dear Reader,

Thank you so much for spending your valuable free time with my fiction and I hope you've enjoyed the crazy ride along with Sara, Teddy, and the gang throughout these three novels! What began as a story I wrote on a whim has turned into a career as a novelist and I couldn't have made it here without your help.

To stay up to date on when I have new fiction available, join my new release mailing list over at ErnieLindsey.com. (You'll also get a free novella by signing up, plus, folks on my list get lots of free fiction and opportunities to get in on early sales.)

As you've probably seen me request in the past, nothing helps a writer more than word of mouth. Please consider leaving a review and sharing with your friends and family on your social networks. It doesn't have to be much. Even a couple of sentences help!

If you're curious about the insanity that Randall and Mary had to go through, referenced throughout this novel, you can follow their story in The White Mountain.

Or, if that's not your cup o' tea, I have plenty more novels and short stories out there and I invite you to check them out.

Again, thank you. It's been a wonderful journey so far and here's to many more books to come. I'll keep writing if you keep reading!

All best,
Ernie

92042933R00177

Made in the USA
Middletown, DE
04 October 2018